THE KID WHO
★ RAN FOR ★
PRESIDENT

THE KID WHO ★ RAN FOR ★ PRESIDENT

DAN GUTMAN

SCHOLASTIC INC.

New York Toronto London Auckland
Sydney Mexico City New Delhi Hong Kong

ISBN 978-0-545-44213-8

12 11 10 9 8 7 6 5 4 3 2 1   12 13 14 15 16 17/0

Printed in the U.S.A.   40
This edition first printing, June 2012

To the next generation of young leaders.
One of *you* will be president someday.

★ Contents ★

THE KID WHO
★ RAN FOR ★
PRESIDENT

★ Prologue ★

"Hi! My name is Judson Moon. I'm twelve years old and I'm running for president of the YOU-nited States."

That's how I introduced myself to about a zillion people last year. I must have kissed a zillion babies, said a zillion hellos, shaken a zillion hands.

When you shake a zillion hands, you learn the fine art of handshaking. You don't hold the other person's hand too loosely, and you don't squeeze it like you're trying to show them how strong you are either. You grab the hand firmly. Look the other person straight in the eye. One pump does it.

Timing is crucial. You can't let go a millisecond too soon or a millisecond too late.

People respect a good handshake. Do it perfectly, and nothing else you do or say much matters. You've just about got that man or woman's vote.

I got a lot of votes. Enough to make me president of the United States? Well, you can peek at page 156 of this book and find out.

That is, if you're a total weenie with the attention span of a flea.

Or, you can read this book and get the whole story. Me? I'd read the book. But hey, it's your choice. It's a free country, right?

1.
★ King of the Hill ★

It was right after Election Day. Lane Brainard and I were down in his basement shooting pool when we first came up with the idea of a kid running for president.

The TV was on. A bunch of boring grown-ups in suits and ties were sitting around a table. I wasn't paying much attention, but they were jabbering something about what the Democratic Party and the Republican Party are going to have to do if they want to win the election next year.

Ordinarily, I would grab the remote control and switch to something more interesting (to me, the Weather Channel would have been more interesting). But Lane's sort of a weird genius who wants to know everything about everything.

His favorite show is *Meet the Press*! Besides, it *was* his house.

Lane recently moved to Madison — that's the capital of Wisconsin, in case you don't know — with his mom. She had just split up with Lane's dad, who lives in California. Lane and I have only known each other for a little while, but we're getting to be good friends.

"The Democrats have been all messed up since they lost control of Congress," Lane explained as he chalked up his stick. "And the Republicans are entirely clueless."

He smacked the cue ball into the pack and balls scattered across the table. The eleven ball dropped in a corner pocket and Lane walked around the table looking for his next shot.

"Half the time the president doesn't know what he's doing, either," I replied. I don't know much about politics, but I can usually fake it if I have to.

"You know who should be running this country, Moon?" Lane said, lining up his next shot. "A kid."

He stroked the five ball toward the side pocket. It just missed, tapping off the bumper.

Lane looked up at me with a sparkle in his eyes. "Can you imagine that, Moon? A kid running for president of the United States? Think about it. It'll be the next election. And a kid becomes the most powerful person in the world! What a mindblower!"

"That's crazy," I said. "The kid would have to be part of the political system. He'd have to know all the politicians. It takes years to make all the connections."

"You know, politicians aren't picked by a bunch of political cronies in smoke-filled rooms anymore, Moon. It's all computers, image consultants, special interest groups, corporate bundlers, online donations, media experts, and advertising now. They might as well be selling soap."

"Don't you have to be thirty-five years old or something like that to run for president?" I asked. I seemed to remember something from history class.

"There are ways around that," Lane replied casually.

"*You* oughta run, Lane," I said. "You're probably the smartest kid around."

"People don't want a smart president," he said.

"They want a president who makes 'em feel good. If they wanted a smart president, Albert Einstein would have been elected."

"You mean he *wasn't*?"

"Moon, you're a dunce. A lovable dunce."

"I was kidding!" I said. "I knew Einstein was never president. I swear it!"

Suddenly Lane stopped and looked at me.

"Wait a minute, Moon," he said. "Why don't *you* run for president?"

"Very funny, Lane. Funny like a crutch."

"No, I *mean* it."

He had this sort of devilish expression on his face, the kind of face you see in old horror movies when a mad scientist cooks up a secret potion or creates a monster that will help him rule the world.

"Moon, you're *perfect*," Lane said, walking around the table excitedly. "People *like* you. You make 'em laugh. You put 'em at ease. You've got a good presidential name — *Judson Moon*. *President* Moon. You look like an all-American boy. You're tall. You've got good hair. It's even parted on the side like a politician —"

"Yeah, right," I interrupted. "Like Americans are going to elect a guy president because they like his *hair*."

"Ever notice that we've never had a bald President?" Lane pointed out.

I thought about that for a moment. "What about Lyndon Johnson? Wasn't he a little thin on top?"

"He doesn't count," Lane said. "He only became president because John F. Kennedy was assassinated."

"What about Eisenhower?"

Lane backed me against his mom's washing machine and looked me in the eye. "The point is, this is America, Moon," he said excitedly. "The land of opportunity. You know what they say — this is the country where *any* kid can become president. Moon, that kid could be *you*."

"Why do you want me to run for President so badly?"

"When I was little," he said, racking up the balls again, "we used to play this game called King of the Hill. There would be a big mountain of dirt or gravel. All the kids would scramble to the top. Then we'd push each other and try to knock each other down the mountain. The one kid who was still at the top at the end was the king of the hill. I was always small and skinny and the other kids always knocked me down on my face. I was never king of the hill. The president of the United States is sorta like the king of the hill. I guess if I could get you elected, it would be sorta like I was king of the hill, too."

Like I said, Lane is a little weird.

2.
A Mighty Big
★ Can of Worms ★

On the way home from Lane's house, I walked down Jenifer Street and saw June Syers sitting on her porch. That was no big surprise, as June Syers is *always* sitting on her porch.

In fact, if I ever walked by her house and *didn't* see June Syers sitting there, I would rush to call the police because something must be terribly wrong. But there she was, as usual.

"Judson Moon!" she hollered. "You come up here this very minute and have a glass of lemonade with me or I'll tell your momma on you."

I bounded up the steps. June Syers is an old African-American woman I've known since the days she used to babysit for me. She has Parkinson's disease, which makes her hands and legs shake. But her mind still works fine. It's a little hard to understand what she's saying sometimes, but I usually find it's worth the effort to try and figure it out.

"Judson Moon, what are you, in fifth grade now?"

"Sixth."

"Sixth grade!" she marveled. "The perfect grade! When you're in sixth grade, you know everything in the world there is to know. In fourth grade, you know nothin'. In fifth grade, you know nothin'. And then suddenly you hit sixth grade and you know it *all*. Nobody can tell you nothin'. Then a funny thing happens when you get older and become a grown-up."

"What's that, Mrs. Syers?"

"You don't know nothin' again," she said, breaking out in her cackling laugh. "Strangest thing."

The lemonade tasted good and I plopped down in the rocking chair next to Mrs. Syers's wheelchair.

"Who was the first president you voted for, Mrs. Syers?"

"Franklin Dellllllllllano Roosevelt!" she said, drawing out the middle name so it sounded almost musical. "And you know who was the *last* president I voted for?"

"Who?"

"Franklin Dellllllllllano Roosevelt!" she said just as proudly.

"You haven't voted since . . ."

"Since 1944."

"Why not?"

"Haven't come across anybody *worth* votin' for since FDR," she said, shaking her head.

"Truman? Eisenhower? Kennedy? Reagan? Obama? None of them were worth voting for?"

"Not in my book. Politicians. Poll takers. When a man — or woman — comes along who *really* wants to lead this country and not just play politics, then I'll pull the lever for 'em. Till then, I'll sit here on this porch and watch the world go down the toilet."

I drained the glass and set it down on the railing. "Mrs. Syers," I said, sticking out my hand, "my name is Judson Moon. I'm twelve years old and I'm running for president."

"What, of your student council or somethin'?"

"No. Of the YOU-nited States of America!"

"You crazy! Even when you were a toddler you were crazy. I still remember the time you hid my glasses in the pan and I baked 'em right into the cake."

"I'm not kidding, Mrs. Syers. I'm thinking I might actually do it."

"Politics changes a person," she said, pointing her bony finger at me. "It rips your heart out and puts a stone in its place."

"Not mine."

As I bounded down her steps, she cupped her hands around her mouth and called out to me. "You're openin' a mighty big can of worms, Judson Moon!"

3.
★ **That Jerk Arthur Krantz** ★

I was sitting around the lunchroom at school with Lane and a bunch of kids. Everybody was talking about what they were going to do on New Year's Eve.

"Man, I'm gonna party all night," said Spencer Bergeron. "We gotta watch the ball fall down, right?"

"It's just another night," Ashley King said. "I'll be playing video games."

"I know what I'm gonna do," I said. "I'm going to be campaigning to be president of the United States."

Everybody busted out laughing.

"Oh yeah, I'm sure," said Merrick Jorgensen. "And I'm gonna fly to the moon on a unicycle blindfolded."

"He's not kidding," Lane chimed in. "He's really going to run for president."

Somebody at the next table turned around to face us. It was Arthur Krantz, president of the Future Lawyers of America Club and just about every other dorky club in school.

If anybody looked like he was running for president, it was Arthur Krantz. He even wears a tie to school on days we don't have assembly.

When we were younger, all the kids called him "Smarty Pants Artie Krantz." Now, of course, we're much more mature. We call him "Booger Boy." I don't even want to get into the reason why.

Arthur was sitting with some other nerds at what we call "The Derf Table." (That's Fred spelled backward.) We used to be friends when I was younger. That was before I figured out what a dweeb he was. He's hated me ever since I told him I didn't want to hang around with him anymore.

"What do you know about the presidency, Moon?" he sneered.

"A lot," I shot back defensively.

"Oh yeah? If the president and the vice president die, who becomes president?"

14

"That's easy," I said. "Chuck Norris."

The kids at my table started giggling.

"Very funny, Moon! If the president and the vice president die, the Speaker of the House becomes president. You should know that."

"And if the Speaker of the House dies," I said loud enough for everyone to hear, "you go to Radio Shack and buy a new speaker."

"Oh, big joke, Moon. Tell me, Mr. President, what do you have to do before you can declare war on another country?"

"I have to call CNN so they can get a camera crew out there right away."

My table was howling. Frank was pounding the table with his fist and tears were streaming down his face. Nothing was funnier than getting Arthur Krantz all steamed up.

Arthur didn't give up. "What's the electoral college, Moon?"

"Everybody knows that. It's where you go to learn how to become an electrician."

"Put an R in the middle of your name and it says what *you* are, Moon — a moron!"

"Well, that doesn't necessarily disqualify me from the presidency, does it, Booger Boy?"

"Thicko!"

"Spasmo!"

"Dappo!"

"Burger-brain!"

"Waste of oxygen!"

By that time, milk was spurting from Ashley's nostrils and Spencer had slid under the table. Arthur got up with his tray and stormed out in a huff.

"I think it would be cool to be president," said Sarah Saladini when we had all regained our composure. "You take limos and helicopters everywhere you go."

"Doesn't the president have his own plane?" Ashley asked.

"Yeah, *Air Force One*," said Lane.

"My family went to Washington last year and we took a tour of the White House," said Sarah. "Did you know it has its own barbershop, a tennis court, a bowling alley, and even a movie theater? The president can watch any movie he wants, anytime he wants."

"Cosmic!" we all agreed.

"And there are six butlers and three chefs. So if the president feels like some food in the middle of the night, he just calls somebody and they bring it to him."

"*Totally* cosmic!"

"That's not why I want to be president," I said, standing up with my tray. "I want to be president so I can bring peace to the world, rescue the environment, and throw out the first ball at baseball games. *Adiós*, amoebas!"

I left them all snickering and throwing napkins in my direction.

After school, Lane started putting the campaign wheels in motion.

The first thing you have to do to run for president, he found out, is to make a petition with signatures of registered voters on it. In Wisconsin, you need 2,000 signatures to get your name on the ballot.

Lane and I went out to the middle of State Street after school and badgered every grown-up we saw until they signed the petition. It took a week to get 2,000 signatures. Lane sent the petition to the Division of Elections and didn't tell them how old I am. A week later I received a letter saying I was on the ballot in Wisconsin.

4.
★ Family Values ★

My folks are pretty oblivious about politics and stuff like that. Let me rephrase that. My folks are just plain oblivious.

Mom is a salesperson for a carpet tile company. She's spent the last twenty years trying to talk businesses into covering their floors with carpet tiles. She must be very persuasive. I see those carpet tiles everywhere. Mom enjoys her work, I suppose. I mean, why would somebody sell carpet tiles for twenty years unless they really liked it?

Dad sells boxes, those corrugated cardboard boxes you pack stuff in when you move. My grandfather sold boxes, too, and when he retired, he passed the business on to Dad.

I think my folks do pretty well. Their cars are always filled with hundreds of carpet tiles and cardboard boxes they have to deliver to customers.

Between the two of them, they know just about everything there is to know about carpet tiles and cardboard boxes. I'm not sure how much they know about anything else. Mostly, they like to talk about carpet tiles and cardboard boxes, which don't interest me all that much.

When they come home from work they're both really beat. It seems like they use up all their thinking at the office so they don't have much energy for thinking at home. I was looking for a chance to break the news to them that I was running for president, and figured I would just casually slip it into the conversation around the dinner table.

The TV was on in the background. The TV is always on in our house, whether anyone's watching it or not. As she ate, Mom was reading a magazine called *Progressive Floor Covering*, which I guess is read by people in the carpet tile business because I never saw any regular people reading it. Dad was absorbed by the latest issue of *Box World Monitor*.

"How was work today?" I asked, trying to get a conversation started.

"Fine, dear," Mom said cheerily from behind her magazine. Dad grunted.

"Mom, Dad, I've given it a lot of thought, and I decided that I'm going to run for president of the United States."

"Not until you mow the lawn you're not," Dad muttered.

"Sure. I'll mow the lawn first. Mom, if I ran for president, would you vote for me?"

"Of course, honey. You know we'd do anything for you."

"Can I borrow five hundred dollars to finance my campaign, Dad?"

"No."

"Did you ever run for anything when you were a kid, Dad?"

"Yeah, the bus."

"So it's okay with you if I run for president?"

"Sure," Dad grunted. "Whatever."

"Hey, Mom, is it okay with you if I go outside and get hit by lightning?"

"As long as nobody gets hurt, dear."

It went on like that for a while. Finally I cleared off my plate and went upstairs to do my homework. Their response wasn't what you'd call wildly enthusiastic, but I did at least have their blessing.

Family values is a big issue at election time, and it was important that my family be behind me.

5.
★ Abby ★

"Yo, stranger!"

I was mowing the lawn when Abby Goldstein called out to me. I released the bar and let the mower sputter to a stop.

"Haven't seen you around much lately," she said.

"I've been pretty busy, Ab."

She looked a little hurt. Abby's my friend and she's a girl, so I guess you could call her my girl-friend. But that's as far as it goes, if you know what I mean.

We've known each other since we were in preschool together, and we've been almost like brother and sister growing up. Since I started hanging out with Lane Brainard lately, I've been seeing less and less of Abby.

"What's up, Judd?" she asked.

"Nothin'. I'm running for president."

"Of the student council?"

"No, of the United States."

Anybody else would think I was kidding, but Abby knew me.

"You are crazy, Judson Moon!" she said, with a big smile on her face. "Remember the time you attached your sled to Andrew Bisgaard's minibike?"

"Yeah, and we knocked down Mrs. Hastings's shed!" We both broke up laughing.

"Don't you have to be a lot older to run for president?" Abby asked.

"Lane says he knows a way around that."

"I'll bet he does." Abby seemed to wrinkle her nose up every time I mentioned Lane.

"You don't like him, do you?"

She sighed. "If you don't have anything nice to say about somebody, you shouldn't say anything at all."

"He's not a bad guy, Ab," I said, "once you get to know him."

"It's okay, Judd. You're allowed to have more than one friend."

"Thanks, Ab."

"By the way, I think you'd make a *wonderful* president, Judson Moon."

"You mean it?"

"Sure I mean it. Politicians are all phonies. It's so obvious that everything they do and say is just to make people vote for them. You're a real person, Judd. People can see it in your eyes when you talk."

I looked into Abby's eyes and put on my zombie face and voice. "You are under my power . . . vote for me . . . I will be your leader . . ."

"Do you really think you can win?"

"Nah! It's just a goof. You know me."

"Remember the time you skateboarded down the center aisle of the auditorium, jumped on the stage, and hit Lindsey in the face with a pie while she was reciting the Gettysburg Address?"

"I was pretending to be John Wilkes Booth," I recalled, laughing.

"The pie got all over her fake beard!"

"I couldn't help it," I said. "It was a once-in-a-lifetime opportunity."

"Anything can happen, you know, Judd. This is America."

"Yeah, what would I do if I actually won the election?"

"If you were president, would we still be friends?"

"Of course," I told her. "We'll always be friends. You know that."

She tightened up her mouth as if she was going to say something but changed her mind just before the words got out.

"I better finish the lawn, Ab." I yanked the cord and the mower sprang to life. "I'll invite you to the White House," I hollered over the roar. "It's got a bowling alley, you know."

As I finished the next row and saw Abby walking away, I noticed she was dabbing her eye with her sleeve.

6.
Secret
★ **Campaign Strategy** ★

Lane passed me a note during social studies class: MEET ME IN THE TREE HOUSE AT 4:00. I nodded back to him and slipped the note in my desk.

Abby and I built the tree house in the woods near my house a few years ago. It wasn't just a bunch of planks nailed to a tree. We hauled in a rug, a couch somebody had thrown away, and an old rocking chair. We even had a battery-operated TV and boom box. It was pretty cool.

Abby and I spent hours up there together. We were both hooked on the game of *Life*, and we'd have these marathon sessions up in the tree.

*   *   *

By the time I climbed the rope ladder to the top, Lane was already up there. He was busily jotting down notes on a long yellow pad.

"I thought this would be a good place for a secret strategy meeting," he said seriously. "We've got a lot we need to talk about."

"Are you sure the tree is secure?" I whispered. "I mean, it might have a bug in it!"

Lane doesn't laugh much, and he didn't laugh at that.

"I liked the way you handled that creep Arthur Krantz in the lunchroom," Lane said. "I was afraid he was going to walk all over you. But you refused to give him a straight answer and made him look like a jerk."

"I thought that only showed how stupid I am."

"No, it *hides* how stupid you are," Lane said. "It's more important for you to *look* as if you know what you're talking about than it is for you to *know* what you're talking about. In a serious discussion of the issues, you're a dead man."

"I know."

"The first thing we need to talk about is me,"

Lane said. "Do you want me to manage this campaign?"

"Sure I do."

"Well, I'll only do it on one condition. I'm in charge. After Election Day, you're in charge. But up until that point, I call the shots. Okay?"

"Sounds fair," I said. What did I know about running for office anyway?

"That means I tell you what to do, what to wear, what to say, and when to say it, Moon. And you've got to run to win. I don't want to get started with this thing unless you're willing to stick with me until the bitter end. So we're in agreement?"

"Let's do it," I said.

To me, the whole thing was a goof. *A kid running for president! That's ridiculous!* But I've certainly done crazier things in my life. In any case, we shook hands on it.

"One of the first things we have to nail down," Lane said, checking off a note on his pad, "is whether you're a Republican or a Democrat."

"How should I know?" I said. "We didn't learn them yet in social studies."

"Well, there are a lot of differences between the two parties. But to put it very simply, the Democrats are in favor of a strong federal government. The Republicans are against putting too much power in the hands of the government."

That meant nothing to me. "What other choices do I have?" I asked.

"Those are the choices! It's a two-party system!"

"But what if I don't like either of those parties?" I complained. "Why can't I just run as me?"

"My feeling exactly," he said, pleased. "Voters are sick of the Democrats and Republicans fighting with each other and never getting anything accomplished. And if you ran as an Independent we wouldn't have to bother with primaries, delegates, conventions, and all that other garbage. Let's run you as an Independent!"

"Great."

"We need a slogan," Lane said, looking up as if one might be written in the sky. "Some catchy line that people will remember. Like 'Keep Cool with Coolidge,' or 'Tippecanoe and Tyler Too.' Something like 'All the Way with LBJ.'"

"How about, 'Vote for Me, I'll Set You Free,'" I volunteered.

"This is a free country, Moon. You don't want to make people feel like they're enslaved."

"How about, 'Moon for President'?"

"Boring."

"How about 'Don't Be a Loon, Vote for Moon'?"

"Catchy, but too silly."

"How about 'Shoot for the Moon'?"

"You want to encourage some crackpot to try and assassinate you?" Lane said.

"How about 'Moon: Let Him Orbit Around You'?"

"Ugh," Lane groaned. "Hey, the moon causes the tides, right? How about 'Moon — He Makes Waves.'"

We both groaned at that one. Neither of us was happy with any of the slogans we were coming up with, so we agreed to put the slogan aside for the moment. Lane looked for the next item on his list.

"We're going to need to pick your running mate," he said.

"Jogging gives me shin splints," I complained.

"Your running mate is your vice presidential candidate, lamebrain."

"Well, why don't *you* be my running mate?"

"I'll have my hands full running your campaign. I can't be vice president, too."

"Oh."

"You want to pick somebody who is very different from yourself. That way, people who don't like you but do like *him* will vote for you anyway."

"Hmmm. What about Arthur Krantz? He's about as different from me as anybody could be."

"Booger Boy? *Nobody* likes that dork," Lane said. "Besides, you and Krantz would kill each other before Election Day."

"How about a grown-up?"

"Good thinking!" Lane said. "Voters who don't want to vote for a kid might feel more comfortable if there was a grown-up on the ticket. Do you have anyone in mind?"

"My dad?"

"You can't have your dad be your vice president!"

I brainstormed for a few minutes, and then it hit me. "I know who would make a good running mate!" I exclaimed. "June Syers!"

"Who's June Syers?" Lane asked.

"You know, that old lady who's always sitting on her porch."

Lane started laughing, and I swear I thought he was going to collapse. He was rolling around clutching his sides and shaking. He almost fell out of the tree house.

Then, suddenly, he stopped laughing. He sat up, said nothing for a few seconds, and announced excitedly, "I love it!"

Lane started scribbling frantically on his pad. "We already have the youth vote. The old lady will give us the African-American vote. She'll give us the senior citizen vote. She'll give us the handicapped vote! And she gives us a killer slogan, too!"

He held up the pad and showed me our first campaign banner . . .

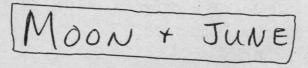

"You're brilliant, Moon! An absolute genius!"

"It was nothing really," I said, polishing an imaginary apple. "I just like her."

We decided that I would talk with Mrs. Syers, and Lane moved down the list to the next item he wanted to discuss.

"We've got to work on your image, Moon."

"What's *wrong* with my image?"

"Don't be so touchy! You don't even have an image yet. We have to *give* you one."

"I thought a person's image was the natural personality they give off."

"You're so naive, Moon," Lane said, shaking his head. "I've been thinking it over and one thing you definitely have to do is change your parakeet's name."

"Change Snot's name?!"

"You can't have a bird named Snot."

"That's her name!"

"It's disgusting!"

"It is Snot!"

"Why'd you name your parakeet Snot in the first place?" Lane asked.

"Well, when we first got her, she was always running around her cage."

"Yeah, so?"

"Like a nose," I explained. "She was always running. And she looks a little bit like a big nose, too."

"So you had to name her Snot? Why didn't you name her Nose or Shnozz? Even Booger would have been a better name."

"I like Snot!"

"How about Cuddles or Choo-Choo?" Lane suggested. "Something voters will find adorable."

I hated the idea of changing Snot's name. But as Lane pointed out, it would be a shame to lose votes just because my parakeet's name offended some people. So Snot became Cuddles.

"Now, our next order of business," Lane said, going down his list. "The First Babe."

"The First Babe?"

"Behind every great man stands a great woman, Moon. You've got to have a First Lady."

"That's a no-brainer, Lane. Abby Goldstein is the First Lady."

Lane took a few moments to find the right words. "Moon, I've given this a lot of thought, and I don't think Abby fits your image."

"I thought you said I don't *have* an image," I blurted out.

"She doesn't fit the image we want to *give* you."

"What's wrong with Abby?"

"Don't take this the wrong way, Moon, but it wouldn't hurt a kid running for the highest office in the country to have a real knockout with him. All those photo opportunities and everything."

I had never thought of Abby as someone who was pretty or not pretty. I just thought of her as my friend.

"You think Abby's ugly?" I asked.

"I didn't say that, Moon. She's just sort of uh . . . normal. Tell me, what do you think of Chelsea Daniels?"

"You mean the girl with the long blond hair in science class? She's the most beautiful girl in the school. Doesn't she do fashion modeling or something?"

"She's the one."

"She doesn't even know who I am," I said.

"Once the word gets around that you're running for president, she'll know who you are. And it will help her modeling career to be seen with you."

"I don't know, Lane. Abby and I have been friends since we were babies. What will she think if some other girl is my First Babe?"

"Moon, you agreed to let me run the campaign and that you'd run to win," Lane said. "I say you get more votes with Chelsea at your side than with Abby at your side. Do me a favor and just *ask* Chelsea. Will you do that for me?"

"Okay," I said reluctantly.

So I had two girls to ask out. June Syers and Chelsea Daniels.

7.
★ The First Babe ★

I spotted Chelsea walking home from school the next day and ran to catch up with her.

"Uh, excuse me, Chelsea?" I said awkwardly from behind.

"Oh, hi! I'm sorry, I don't know your name."

She turned around to face me. Chelsea Daniels is one of those twelve-year-old girls who looks like she's about eighteen in the magazine ads. I know it's not cool to think a girl is beautiful just because she has blond hair and blue eyes, but looking at Chelsea somehow makes the muscles in your face malfunction and you forget how to talk.

"Judson," I finally choked out. "Judson Moon."

"Hi, Judson Moon," she said. I recorded in my mental memory bank that Chelsea Daniels had actually spoken my name. The words "Judson Moon" had passed through her lips.

"Can I ask you a question, Chelsea?"

"I'm kinda in a hurry . . ."

"It'll only take a minute. See, I'm running for president . . ."

"What, of the student council?"

"No. Of the United States."

She stared at me, then laughed. "Yeah?"

"And every president has to have a First Babe. I mean First Lady."

"Yeah . . . ?"

"I was wondering if you might be *my* First Lady."

"Is this going to be on YouTube or something?" she said, looking around for a camera. "Who put you up to this?"

"Nobody." I reached into my backpack and pulled out one of the petitions Lane and I had been circulating. She looked it over.

"We don't have to *date* each other or anything, do we?" Chelsea asked, wrinkling her nose.

"No, of course not!" I assured her. "I might ask you to attend some functions with me. Parties and stuff . . ."

"Parties?!" she said, brightening. "Formal parties where I would get dressed up and there would be photographers and stuff?"

"Possibly," I said.

"Cool!" she said, finally smiling at me like I deserved to be on the same planet as her. "Do you think I would look better in a blue or a pink silk dress at the inauguration?"

It was as simple as that. I had my First Babe.

8.
★ Vice President Syers ★

Talking June Syers into being my vice presidential running mate wouldn't be as easy as talking Chelsea Daniels into being my First Lady.

When I got to Mrs. Syers's stoop, she wasn't there. I was just about to call the police when she wheeled out of her apartment door onto the porch.

"Hey, Mr. President!" she yelled. "How goes the campaign?"

"Mrs. Syers! I was worried. Where were you?"

"Ain't an old lady allowed to use the bathroom?" she complained.

"I want to ask you a serious question, Mrs. Syers."

"A boy your age shouldn't even *have* any serious questions yet."

"Would you consider being my vice president?"

"You crazy, Judson Moon. You *always* been crazy. You were a crazy baby. You're a crazy kid. And you gonna be a crazy grown-up, too."

"Maybe, but I still would like you to be my running mate."

"Judson Moon, ain't you got some homework that needs doin'? Shouldn't you be out playin' ball with your friends? Why do you want to get yourself messed up with this stuff?"

"C'mon, Mrs. Syers. It'll be fun!"

"Fun? Don't you know that bein' president is just about the worst job in the world? Everybody hates you no matter what you do. You can't go anywhere. They watch your every move. You say one wrong word or do one wrong thing and everybody jumps all over you. Then in four years they kick you out on your behind. Maybe eight. What do you need that for?"

"I don't expect to win or anything," I explained. "I just think it will be a hoot to run for president. And I can't think of anyone I'd rather do it with than you, Mrs. Syers."

"Ain't never been a lady vice president."

"There's never been a twelve-year-old president, either," I pointed out. "Everything that's ever been done had to be done by somebody *first*, didn't it?"

"Why do you want me, anyhow? Why don't you pick some pretty boy politician?"

"Because you're the only grown-up I know who isn't stupid," I admitted.

"Well, you're right about that. But I'm too old. Maybe thirty years ago . . ."

"You are *not* too old. You're strong as an ox. And thirty years ago a female candidate would have been a joke. But now there are lots of them."

"You don't take no for an answer, do you, Judson Moon?"

"No."

"Oh, all right. Vice presidents don't do nothin' more than sit on a porch anyway. And somebody's gotta keep an eye on you, Judson Moon. I been doin' it all your life. Lord knows your momma ain't never home."

"So you'll do it?"

"I'll do it. I'll do it."

"Mrs. Syers, I could kiss you!"

"Save it for election night, Romeo."

And so I had my First Lady and my running mate.

9.
Twenty Million Dollars?
★ No Problem. ★

"It's time to talk turkey," Lane said as we settled into the couch in my basement for our next strategy session. He was thrilled that Chelsea agreed to be my First Lady and June Syers said she'd be my running mate. But he had other things on his mind.

"We're going to need money," Lane said. "A *lot* of money."

"I've got about two hundred dollars in my savings account," I offered. I was saving that money up to buy a video game system, and hoped Lane would tell me we wouldn't need it.

"You're kidding, right?" he said. "You think you can run for president on two hundred bucks?"

"Maybe I can borrow a little more from my folks."

"Two hundred dollars won't even buy you a good *suit*, Moon!"

"Wait a minute," I interrupted. "You didn't tell me I would have to wear a suit."

"Of *course* you've got to wear a suit. Presidential candidates *always* wear suits."

"I *hate* suits," I complained. "I had to wear a suit for my uncle's wedding. It was awful."

"Then you've already got a suit."

"So I don't have to buy one. That's two hundred dollars we saved right there."

"Moon, we're gonna need twenty million."

"Twenty million . . . *dollars*?" I gulped.

"That's just to get started. We'll need more as we get closer to Election Day."

"What costs so much that we need that kind of money?"

Lane ticked off all the things that cost money in an election campaign — commercial time on TV and radio, airfare, office space, staff, telephone bills, printing. Plus bumper stickers, T-shirts, balloons, banners. I guess that's why you don't see poor people running for president.

"Hey, I've got an idea," I said enthusiastically. "Why don't we get a sponsor for the campaign?"

"What do you mean, a sponsor?"

"You know, like McDonald's or Nike or some other big company. They give us twenty million dollars and I could tell people to eat at McDonald's."

"Are you out of your mind, Moon? What are you going to say at your inauguration — I do solemnly swear that I will faithfully execute the Office of President of the United States, and everybody should eat more Egg McMuffins?"

"Athletes endorse stuff," I said sheepishly.

"Well, politicians don't. At least not legally."

"Wasn't Herbert Hoover sponsored by that vacuum cleaner company?"

"Hoover was his *name*, brainless!"

"Lighten up, Lane. I was kidding about Hoover. So we need a lot of people giving a little money each, right?"

"Now you're getting it. And it's got to add up to about twenty million."

"Oh, well, I didn't want to be president so badly anyway."

"You give up too easily, Moon. I know how we can raise twenty million dollars with two phone calls."

10.
I'd Say It Sounds
★ Like a Fake ★

Lane opened up his laptop and Googled "The Cap Times," which is the name of our local newspaper. He found the phone number, picked up the phone, and started to dial. I noticed he had a copy of the paper next to him on the couch. I didn't know what he was up to.

As the phone was ringing, he motioned for me to go into another room and pick up an extension.

"*Capital Times,*" a lady answered after almost ten rings.

"Give me the news desk, please," Lane said.

"I'll connect you."

"News," a gruff male voice said after the transfer was made.

"May I speak with Pete Guerra, please?" Lane asked.

"Where's Guerra?" the guy shouted. "Guerra, phone!" He put the receiver down and I could hear the buzz of a newsroom in the background.

Finally, another guy came to the phone. "Guerra here. Whatsup?"

"Mr. Guerra," Lane said in his most grown-up voice, "I saw your article about the baby seals in the paper today and wanted to tell you that you did a terrific job."

"What are you, ten years old?" Pete Guerra didn't sound impressed by the compliment.

"I'm twelve," Lane said.

"Kid, I'm on a deadline. Whaddya want?"

"I think I have a story for you, Mr. Guerra."

"What are ya sellin'?"

"I'm not selling anything."

"Kid, *everybody's* selling something. You might as well learn that while you're young."

"Mr. Guerra, what would you say if I told you there was a boy my age who is running for the office of president of the United States?"

"I'd say it sounds like a fake. Sonny, if you like pranks, why don't you call Pizza Hut and tell them to deliver a pie to the house across the street from you? 'Cause I got a lot of work to do."

"You'd have less work if you followed this story and won a Pulitzer Prize in journalism."

"Okay, kid," Guerra said wearily. "Don't tell me, let me guess. You're runnin' for president because you think it'll get you an A in social studies, right?"

"I'm not running. The candidate is a remarkable young gentleman named Judson Moon. He's in sixth grade at the Georgia O'Keeffe Middle School right here in Madison, and he's quite serious about his candidacy. He already has two thousand signatures on a petition, which qualifies him to be on the ballot in Wisconsin next November."

"One problem, kid," Guerra said. "Ever read the Constitution? Kids aren't *allowed* to be president."

"Oh yeah?" said Lane. "Well, women and African-Americans used to not be allowed to vote."

"Who are you, the kid's campaign manager?"

"As a matter of fact, I am. My name is Lane Brainard, spelled just the way it sounds. I think Moon's bid for the presidency is a great human interest story, Mr. Guerra. It's at *least* as interesting as a bunch of baby seals."

"Hey, don't knock the seals," Guerra warned. "They lost their mother."

"And when Judson Moon wins the election in November, you're going to feel pretty dumb for not breaking the story when you had the chance. Because, Mr. Guerra, as you and I both know, everybody's selling something. What you're selling is your reputation as a journalist. And the story of a kid running for president of the United States will be the biggest story of your career."

Man, Lane was smooth. Guerra didn't say anything for a moment or two.

"Put Moon on the phone," he finally barked.

"Mr. Moon is unavailable to speak right now. But he will give you an exclusive interview if you come to 301 Spaight Street tomorrow morning at ten. Unless, of course, you've got to cover another animal story . . ."

"I'll be there," Guerra said.

"Good. You might want to bring a camera with you. It will be a nice photo opportunity."

"Hey, kid?"

"Yes?"

"I like your chutzpah."

"Thank you."

I ran into the den as soon as they hung up the phone. "Man, you were awesome!" I told Lane. "What's chutzpah?"

"How should I know? The important thing is, he's gonna be here tomorrow."

"But there's one thing I don't understand, Lane. How is this gonna get us twenty million dollars?"

"You'll see," he said with a gleam in his eye. "You'll see."

11.
★ The Lemonade Party ★

It was a bright, sunny Saturday morning. Lane showed up at nine o'clock, wheeling June Syers, who was holding an enormous basket of lemons on her lap.

My folks were already gone for the day, attending seminars to help them sell more carpet tiles and cardboard boxes.

"I hate suits," I said, pulling at my collar.

"You look outstanding," Lane said. "Very presidential."

Lane and I set up a long table at the edge of the lawn and Mrs. Syers got to work making lemonade.

I dug some long sticks of wood out of the basement and nailed cardboard to them. Lane has nicer handwriting than I do, so he painted three

signs: MOON & JUNE FOR PRESIDENT, HELP US!; WE
NEED $20 MILLION!; and LEMONADE 25 CENTS.

"Twenty million dollars?" whistled Mrs. Syers.
"I'm gonna need more lemons."

"It's just a symbol," Lane explained, blowing
up balloons to hang on the booth. "Grown-ups
get all misty-eyed when they see lemonade
stands. It reminds 'em of the good old days."

"There *were* no good old days," harrumphed
Mrs. Syers. "The good old days is anything that
happens before you're old enough to see the
world as it really is."

I live on a pretty busy street. Cars started pulling over right away and soon our lemonade stand
was surrounded by people.

"Hi!" I said to each person cheerfully. "My
name is Judson Moon. I'm twelve years old and
I'm running for president of the YOU-nited States."

"Keep smiling," Lane whispered in my ear.
"And don't say anything that will make anybody
angry. Kiss some babies."

"I'm not really into kissing," I complained. "Do
I have to?"

"Then hug people."

"I'm not very good at it," I admitted. "I never know which side I should put my head. If I put my head toward the left and if the other person puts her head toward the right, we bump heads. Can't I just punch 'em on the arm?"

We never had the chance to solve the problem. A beat-up PT Cruiser pulled up, followed by a minivan. A sloppily dressed guy got out of the Cruiser. He was carrying a pad in his hand and a pencil behind his ear.

"Judson Moon?" he said, sticking out his hand. "My name is Pete Guerra, with the *Cap Times*. I figured you wouldn't mind if I brought a few of the TV newsboys with me."

A couple of guys got out of the minivan lugging video cameras, still cameras, a tripod, tape recorder, and microphone. They took a bunch of pictures of me serving people lemonade, and then Lane ushered us off to the side so Pete Guerra could interview me.

"So why ya running for president, kid?"

"Well, I figure grown-ups have had the last one thousand years to mess up the world. Now it's our turn."

"That's a good quote," Guerra said, looking up from the pad he was scribbling on. "Did you think of that yourself or did your campaign manager feed it to you?"

"Lane's job is to run the campaign," I explained. "My job, as a candidate for the highest office in our nation, is to come up with good quotes."

"Ya got any pets, kid?"

"A parakeet," I replied. "Her name is Sn — Cuddles," I lied.

"Okay, let's get down to more serious business, Judson. People are going to want to know what positions you take."

"I play third base," I said. "Sometimes I'll play the outfield if the coach needs me out there."

Guerra rolled his eyes and shook his head from side to side. "No, I mean your positions on the *issues*. Your *opinions*. Like, what do you think about gun control?"

"Guns don't kill people. They usually just cause serious injuries."

"What about race?"

"I love all the races. My dream is to see the Indianapolis 500 and the Kentucky Derby someday."

"What's the first thing you plan to do when you become president?"

"Install a skateboard ramp in the Oval Office and redecorate the White House with hip-hop posters."

"When did you decide to run for president, Judson?"

"When I found out the White House had a bowling alley."

When Guerra had enough of my wisecracks, he moved over to June Syers, who was dispensing her worldview for free with every cup of lemonade.

"Mrs. Syers," asked Guerra. "How did you become Judson Moon's running mate?"

"Musta been my good looks and sparkling personality," she said.

"Does Moon have what it takes to lead the country?"

"He can't hardly do any worse than the fools who are runnin' it now, can he?" she said. Then she proceeded to give him a capsule history of the United States, which basically consisted of saying the Indians were fools, the Pilgrims were fools, the Founding Fathers were fools, the Union and the Confederacy were fools, and every politician except Franklin D. Roosevelt was a fool.

"And I oughta know," she concluded, " 'cause I lived through all of 'em."

As soon as Guerra and the TV guys left, Lane began tearing down our stand. Mrs. Syers counted up the money, and proudly announced that we had raised sixty-five dollars. There was a lot more lemonade we could have sold, but Lane wasn't interested.

"The idea wasn't to sell lemonade," he said. "The idea was to make news. The money will come later."

12.
Homework First,
★ Campaigning Later ★

"Turn on channel three!" Lane shouted breathlessly into the phone that night while I was eating dinner.

Dad and Mom didn't seem to be paying attention to the TV, so I switched channels.

"After these messages," the anchorman bellowed, "we'll tell you about a twelve-year-old boy who says he's running for president. Stay tuned."

"Where do they get these stupid stories?" Dad muttered from behind his newspaper.

I didn't say a word. I wanted to see the look on his face. After three commercials, the news anchor came back on.

"Well, they say that in America any youngster can grow up to be president. But at least one youngster isn't going to wait. Twelve-year-old

Judson Moon of Madison is throwing his baseball cap into the ring right *now*."

Mom and Dad actually lowered their newspapers and looked at the TV. My face filled the screen and Dad's jaw fell open. Mom dropped the glass she was holding and it shattered on the floor.

"Grown-ups have had the last one thousand years to mess up the world," I heard myself say. "Now it's our turn."

"Moon will be running as a third party candidate representing 'The Lemonade Party' for the presidency in November," the anchorman continued. "The sixth grader and his running mate — an elderly African-American woman named June Syers — have already collected the two thousand signatures they need to get on the ballot in Wisconsin, and they're raising money by selling lemonade at a stand in front of Judson's house. We asked Mr. Moon how he plans to get around the Constitution, which clearly states that a candidate must be thirty-five years of age to run for the presidency."

"I'm actually thirty-six," I said to the camera

with a smirk. "I'm just extremely young for my age."

"That's our news for tonight. Good night and may all *your* news be good news."

Before Mom or Dad could say a word, the phone rang. It was my aunt Lucy.

"Am I hallucinating!?" she shrieked. "Or did I just see you on TV?"

The instant I hung up the phone with Aunt Lucy, it rang again. It was one of my teachers. When I hung up with her, the phone rang again. Kids from school were calling. Mom's friends were calling. Total strangers were calling. Finally, Dad took the phone off the hook.

"Is this one of your pranks?" he asked. I wasn't sure if he was angry or amused.

"It's *sort* of a prank," I replied. "I don't expect to win or anything. You're always telling me I should get involved with extracurricular activities. Well . . ."

"I meant you should join the chess club or the school paper or something!" he said, his voice rising. "I didn't mean you should run for president!"

"Why didn't you tell us, dear?" asked Mom.

"I *did* tell you, Mom. You just weren't listening."

"Well, I think it's cute, honey," she said, "as long as it doesn't interfere with your school-work. Remember, homework first, running for president second."

Dad just rolled his eyes and shook his head slowly from side to side.

13.
★ A Star Is Born ★

In the morning, I got up early and rushed outside to get the paper. There I was on the front page, with this big smile on my face, pouring some lady a cup of lemonade. There was an article to go with the photo:

MOON MISSION: 12-YEAR-OLD ON QUEST FOR WHITE HOUSE
By Pete Guerra

While other boys his age are flipping baseball cards and dyeing their hair purple, Judson Moon has other things on his mind — like running for president of the United States.

The 12-year-old from Madison says he is disillusioned with the Republicans and Democrats and has decided to mount a campaign as a third-party candidate in November's election.

"Grown-ups have had the last one thousand years to mess up the world," claims Moon. "Now it's our turn."

The young man, outfitted in a suit and tie, was raising money on Saturday by selling lemonade in front of his house for 25 cents a cup. He will have to sell 80 million cups to raise $20 million, the figure he says he needs to mount a national campaign.

Moon's running mate and fellow lemonade saleswoman is Mrs. June Syers, a retired nurse who used to babysit for the candidate.

"We're a perfect team," Moon says. "I'm young and she's old. I'm white and she's black. I'm dumb and she's smart."

Watch out, Democrats and Republicans! Stand back, Tea Partiers! Here comes The Lemonade Party!

Word gets around fast. When I walked into school on Monday morning, it was like I was from another planet. Everywhere I went, everybody was looking at me, pointing, and whispering. I'd walk toward a crowd of kids and they'd part to let me through.

Pretty weird!

Abby wished me good luck. Several of the teachers gave me the thumbs-up sign. Even Chelsea came over to me.

"You weren't kidding about running for president, were you?" she said, a lot friendlier than she was when we met.

"No, I wasn't," I replied. "You weren't kidding about being First Lady, were you?"

"Actually I *was*," she said. "But now that I know you're really doing this, you can count on me."

Arthur Krantz made a face when he saw me, and I made the same face right back at him. As every politician knows, you can't please all the people all the time.

At first I didn't like all the attention, but by lunchtime I had changed my mind and decided that it was kinda cool. I could definitely get used to being a celebrity.

I was signing an autograph for some third grader at my locker when Principal Berlin came over to me. I had never met the man, as it's always been my policy to stay away from principals as much as possible. But he stuck out his hand and congratulated me.

"Mr. Moon," he said, clapping me on the back. "You are a credit to O'Keeffe School. I wish all the students had your ambition. Listen, Judson, I was wondering if you would address the school at the assembly tomorrow morning. You can kick off your campaign right here at O'Keeffe."

"I'm . . . speechless," I stammered.

"Well, I hope you won't be tomorrow!" he chortled. With that, he turned on his heel and ambled down the hall.

I grabbed Lane in the cafeteria.

"I'm in big trouble!" I told him. "Berlin wants me to give a speech at assembly tomorrow!"

"Great!" was Lane's reaction.

"But the only time I ever spoke in front of a group, it was my parents. And they weren't even listening! What am I gonna do?"

"Don't worry!" Lane said reassuringly. "You think politicians make up their own speeches? I'll write a dynamite speech for you. All you have to do is read it."

"But I'm not even a good reader!" I complained.

"Relax! This is perfect. It's a small school setting. A friendly crowd. This will give you the opportunity to get used to making speeches. Judd, everything is going to be okay."

That was easy for *him* to say. He didn't have to

stand up on the stage all by himself with three hundred and fifty kids staring at him.

I had started this whole running for president thing as a joke. But like all jokes, it was getting less funny the more I heard it.

14.
Give the People
★ What They Want ★

JUDSON MOON FOR PRESIDENT read the huge banner strung across the stage. It looked like every American flag in the school had been moved into the auditorium. I peeked from behind the curtain and saw my classmates sitting out there, buzzing with excitement. The school band was playing "Hail to the Chief." The podium looked like a lonely place to be.

Lane straightened my tie for me and handed me some sheets of paper.

"What does it say?" I asked.

"It's a pretty standard political speech," he replied. "You know, the flag, patriotism. Stuff like that."

"I'm scared, Lane. What am I doing here?"

"Starting the adventure of a lifetime," he said with a smile. "You'll be great. Can you feel the energy out there? Feed off it! Throw their energy right back at them!"

I didn't have any time to read Lane's speech. Principal Berlin got up onstage. He held his hand up and made the V-sign with his fingers, which in our school means everybody has to stop talking right away.

"Students," the principal said when everybody calmed down, "I have been at O'Keeffe School for eighteen years. In that time I have met many remarkable young men and women. But never in my years here have I run across a student with the ambition of this young man. I asked him here today to give his first public speech and kick off his campaign. I hope he will be an example to you all. Let's give a big hand for the next president of the United States, our own . . . Judson Moon!"

Lane gave me a little shove and I walked to the podium.

The applause was deafening. I've heard applause before, of course. But never for *me*. When the applause is for *you*, it somehow sounds different. You hear the hands clapping with your ears, but it just washes over you. You can't tell how loud it is or how long it goes on. You go into a sort of trance state.

Finally, the kids hushed themselves. The whole school was staring at me. I fumbled for the papers Lane had given me. It took all my concentration to read the words. It didn't matter what they said. I just didn't want to make any dumb mistakes.

"Fellow students," I began, "we are making history today. Never, in the history of the United States of America, has a *child* — one of *us* — run for the office of president. That's what I am doing, and I come here today to ask for your support."

Some kids started cheering and hooting. A chant of "MOON! MOON! MOON! MOON!" swept across the auditorium. The teachers did their best to shush the kids. I waited until everybody calmed down before continuing.

"I'm sure you're aware of the problems our country faces today. Crime. Climate change. Unemployment. Racism. Substance abuse. Too much homework . . ."

That got a laugh.

"Let me ask you this," I continued. "Who is responsible for these problems? Is it Congress?

Foreigners? Rich people? Poor people? Black people? White people? Women? Men? No, there is one group who is totally to blame for all the problems in our country today, and I'll tell you who that group is."

I paused for a moment to find my place on the page.

"Grown-ups!" I shouted.

The kids went nuts. A cheer went up. Kids were stomping their feet. The teachers began to look around at each other nervously.

"*That's* who's responsible for the problems of our country. Tell me, who's responsible for housing discrimination, sex discrimination, and race discrimination?"

"Grown-ups!" they screamed.

"Who burned all the fossil fuels, cut down the rain forests, made our water unsafe to drink, and our air unsafe to breathe?"

"Grown-ups!" they screamed even louder.

"Who brought on the health care crisis?"

"Grown-ups!"

"Who caused every war in the history of this planet?"

"Grown-ups!"

"That's right! Kids had nothing to do with *any* of these problems. Tell me this — are grown-ups going to solve all these problems they created?"

"No!" the whole school shouted.

"That's right," I said, more confidently. "In this young millennium, it's gonna be up to *us* to solve the problems created in the last millennium. And the way I look at it, the first step is for a kid to run for president. And win!"

They were in the palm of my hand now. I could feel it. Every student was silent and staring at me, even the eighth-grade jerks who *never* shut up for anything. I felt like I could tell them that the earth was really flat and they'd agree with me.

I spotted Chelsea in the front row. She was looking at me in awe.

"Now, we all know that none of us can vote yet," I continued. "The grown-ups made sure of that, didn't they? What I want each of *you* to do is convince your parents to vote for *me*. You may have to beg them. You may have to put a little pressure on them. But if you want to solve these problems I've been talking about, do whatever you can to get your moms and dads to vote for me. Because if they vote for another grown-up, we'll only have the same old problems grown-ups have caused over the last two centuries."

"MOON! MOON! MOON! MOON! MOON! MOON!" they chanted. It took a while before I could continue.

"My fellow students, I know what you're thinking. You're thinking, 'What's in it for *me*?' Well, I'll *tell* you what's in it for you. In appreciation for your support, my first official act as president of the United States will be to abolish homework, now and forever!"

A huge roar of approval went up across the auditorium. Clapping. Screaming. Foot stomping. The whole room was shaking. It felt like a football game. The teachers were flipping out.

I felt an exhilarating surge of power I had never experienced before. They were cheering because of *me*. They were whipped up because of what *I* was saying. It was a rush.

"If your parents vote for me," I bellowed into the microphone, "homework will go the way of the horse and buggy."

Fists were pumping in the air.

"Homework will become a quaint reminder of what life was like back in our parents' childhoods!"

Kids were jumping up and down on their seats.

"In our childhood, the only place you'll see homework will be in museums!"

It was pandemonium. I paused to allow them to calm down a little. I didn't want to incite a riot or anything.

I noticed a boy standing in the middle of the auditorium, raising his hand and shouting insistently, "Excuse me!" Peering at him, I could see it was that jerk Arthur Krantz.

"Yes, Mr. Krantz," I called out. "You have a comment?"

"First of all, the president of the United States has no power to abolish homework. None. Zero. Second, we *need* homework. Doing homework is how students reinforce what we learn at school! Homework is a *good* thing."

I glanced over to Lane at the side of the stage for some advice. He was mouthing some words to me, but I couldn't make them out. I was never any good at reading lips. But watching him gave me an idea.

"READ MY LIPS, BOOGER BOY!" I bellowed. "NO . . . MORE . . . HOMEWORK!"

"NO MORE HOMEWORK! NO MORE HOMEWORK! NO MORE HOMEWORK!" chanted the school as one. The kids around Krantz told him to shut up and sit down.

"You're just making empty promises to get votes!" Krantz shouted at me. "Your candidacy is a joke! Your running mate is a grown-up, you hypocrite! You don't know anything about *any-thing*. You're going to make all kids look bad!"

A group of boys jumped on Krantz and started punching him. Some teachers rushed over to pull the boys off him. Krantz was taken out of the auditorium holding his hand over his eye.

I glanced at my speech and saw I was almost at the bottom.

"Fellow students, our grandparents had their chance to save America. They blew it! Our parents had their chance to save America. They blew it! Now it's a new millennium and our generation is going to get our chance. Let's not blow it! The time has come to pass the torch to a new generation. Ask not what your parents can do for you. Ask what *you* can do for yourselves! Kids are the only hope for America. Thank you."

"NO MORE HOMEWORK!" the kids chanted as I left the podium. "NO MORE HOMEWORK!"

As I came off the stage, Principal Berlin looked at me like I was an insect. The teachers looked like they were in shock.

The kids, of course, looked thrilled. The dumbest guys seemed particularly happy, fist bumping me and saying stuff like, "Awesome, dude."

"Looks as if you've got the kids' vote," Lane said, giving me a hug.

"Don't you think that went a little too far, Lane?" I asked. "Krantz was right, you know. I can't promise to get rid of homework! That's crazy!"

"It's the first rule of politics, Judd. Give the people what they want."

Lane led me over to a guy waiting backstage. "Judson," he said, "I want to introduce you to Ben Davis. He's with the AP."

"Pleased to meet you," I said as I shook the guy's hand. "My mom does her grocery shopping at your store."

"Not the A&P, Judd," Lane said, chuckling. "The A-P. Associated Press."

"Which paper is that?" I asked.

"All of them," Davis replied. "When I write a story, the AP puts it in hundreds of newspapers. Sometimes thousands. And we blast it out to every news web site on the net."

"Wow!" I marveled. "And they haven't been caught?"

He thought that was funny.

"Not every newspaper and web site creates their own content," Davis said. "They pay a guy like me to write something once, and then they run it everywhere. That's called syndication."

"Are you going to write an article about me that will run everywhere?" I asked.

"You got it, kid. You're going to be all over the news tomorrow morning."

I gulped. Lane was beaming from ear to ear. He was taking this run for president *seriously*. He must have taken the clipping that appeared in the *Capital Times* and sent it to the Associated Press.

One day I was a fairly anonymous kid who liked to ride his bike and go fishing. The next day, virtually every man, woman, and child in America would know my name.

15.
★ America Is Calling ★

The instant I opened my eyes the next morning, I knew my life would never be the same.

The phone rang at 5:30. A lady asked if I was Judson Moon. When I told her I was, she said, "Judson, I'm Ann Curry with *The Today Show*. Could I talk with you live on the air this morning?"

"Very funny," I said groggily, and hung up the phone. It was too early for practical jokes.

But as soon as the receiver hit the cradle, the phone rang again.

"Judson Moon?" a woman's voice asked. "The boy who's running for president?"

"Yes?"

"I'm Rebecca Gardner, talent coordinator with *The Tonight Show*. Would you be available to appear on our program tomorrow night?"

"I don't know," I mumbled. "I have a lot of homework this week."

"We'll charter a flight for you," she offered. "First class hotel. Limousine. Would you like to visit Disneyland while you're here? I can arrange that."

"Can you call me back in five minutes?" I asked.

I hung up the phone and it rang again.

"Judson, this is Ann Curry again. Listen, I'm sorry I woke you up. But it's a morning show and we have to get going pretty early . . ."

"Call back in five minutes!" I snapped at her.

I wanted to get Lane on the phone, but every time I put down the receiver, the phone would ring again.

Somebody from *People* magazine called saying they wanted to put me on the cover. *The National Enquirer* wanted to buy the rights to my life story. Finally I was able to speed-dial Lane.

"You gotta get over here!" I practically shouted into the phone. "America is calling!"

"The Associated Press story must have hit the papers," he said. "I'll be right over. Let me handle everything."

I hung up the phone and it rang again. It was Mrs. Syers. She complained that *TMZ* had woken her up at five o'clock in the morning begging to interview her.

I took the phone off the hook while waiting for Lane to bike over to my house. Mom and Dad rushed out to work before I had the chance to ask them if I could stay home from school. Lane wheeled into the driveway right after my folks pulled out of it.

The phone rang about a second after we put the receiver back on the cradle.

"Moon campaign headquarters," Lane answered matter-of-factly.

Everybody who was anybody was trying to get through. *Sixty Minutes* wanted me and Mrs. Syers on the show. MTV wanted to follow me around for a day with their cameras and turn my life into a reality TV show. Some Japanese TV station was willing to fly an entire camera crew to America to interview me. Ann Curry called again.

Lane cut a deal with a big New York publisher for my life story. He told Pepsi I don't do commercial endorsements. Watching Lane work the phone was like watching a master potter mold a vase out of clay.

When the smoke had cleared, Mrs. Syers and I were scheduled to appear on *The Today Show, The Tonight Show, The Late Show, The Daily Show,* and *Good Morning America.* I would be on the cover of *People, Sports Illustrated for Kids, Time,* and *Boys' Life.*

Hardball wanted me to go on their show, but only if I didn't appear on any other TV shows. Lane told them to buzz off. He turned down requests from the TV shows, magazines, and bloggers he never heard of.

"Why did you turn down *Meet the Press*?" I asked Lane. "I thought that was your favorite show."

"You're not ready to meet the press," he replied.

In the middle of all this, I managed to get through to school and tell them I wouldn't be coming in. I told the secretary I had a funny feeling in the pit of my stomach, which was absolutely true. She had read the papers, and said she thought everybody would understand.

By ten o'clock, reporters started gathering out on the front lawn, setting up cameras and

satellite hookups. Some guy was trying to interview me with a bullhorn. I pulled the shades
down. It was like *Night of the Living Dead*, when
the zombies are trying to claw their way into the
house.

We decided to let just one reporter in — Pete
Guerra, the guy who came out to the lemonade
stand and wrote the first story about my run for
the presidency.

"The power of the press," muttered Guerra
after pushing his way through the mob of reporters and through the front door. "You're gonna
have to reseed your lawn, Moon. Reporters are
worse than animals."

Pete sat down on the living room couch and
asked a few questions. When he was finished,
he asked me if I would mind a little friendly
advice. I told him I would appreciate any tips he
might have.

"You kids are new at this," he said. "Lots of
people want you, Moon. But there's something
you should know. Nobody out there is your
friend. Everybody wants a piece of you. To sell
newspapers or magazines. To improve their TV

or radio ratings, or get suckers to click on their web site. To make money. All I'm sayin' is, be careful. Don't trust *anybody*. America chews up celebrities and spits 'em out. I hate to see a nice kid like you get burned."

I thanked Pete for the advice. It was obvious that he was more than just a reporter. I could count on him as a friend.

As Pete pushed his way out the door and through the throng of reporters and cameramen on the front lawn, I spotted Gus, our mailman. Lane and I ushered him inside.

"They say dogs with rabies are dangerous!" Gus said, handing me a thick stack of letters. "Some guy just offered me fifty bucks to give you a note."

"What did you tell him, Gus?"

"I told him he could get it here a lot cheaper if he'd just put a stamp on it."

Usually the mail is a bunch of catalogs and coupons and other junk. But the pile of mail Gus handed me was a bunch of letters in regular-size envelopes with my name and address written on them by hand. I pulled out one envelope and ripped it open.

Dear Judson Moon,

I am in fourth grade. I read in the paper that you are running for president and I think that's just about the coolest thing that a kid my age would run for president. You're an inspiration to millions of kids like me. I made a lemonade stand just like you and raised $34.25 in a morning. I want you to have the money to help you run.

Good luck!

Johnny Fishman

A check for $34.25 fluttered to the ground. I ripped open another envelope. It was from a kid in Arkansas who put up a lemonade stand. $52.50 in bills and change tumbled out.

Lane and I put all the envelopes on the floor and started furiously ripping them open. There were about fifty of them. Some were simply addressed JUDSON MOON, MADISON, WISCONSIN.

Some of the letters were from kids who put up lemonade stands. Other kids had car washes, bake sales, or yard sales. Kids were actually selling their own *toys* to raise money for me!

With each letter was a check or a bunch of bills. The largest contribution was $103.

We counted up all the money and it came to $2,568.75. We felt like we had won the lottery.

"You're a genius," I told Lane.

"And *you*," Lane said, clapping a hand on my back, "are becoming America's hero."

16.
The Customer Is
★ Always Right ★

In the next few days, Americans must have guzzled a lot of lemonade. Poor Gus showed up at the door with an enormous sackful of envelopes. He looked like Santa Claus. Money and gifts poured in from all over the country.

Deep in the pile was a card that said I had a package waiting for me at the post office, and that I should come get it right away. I went over there to pick it up and the package was a dog — a little cocker spaniel I named Chester. I always wanted a dog, so at least *something* came out of running for president.

Lane took care of all the details. He opened a bank account and carefully recorded each donation. He rented office space and coordinated volunteers to run it. An artist was hired to draw a picture of the moon with a photo of my face in the middle of it. The logo was used on our bumper stickers, T-shirts, buttons, and flyers.

The campaign was picking up speed, and Chelsea was acting more and more friendly to me at school. She came up to me at my locker one day and said she had something important she wanted to talk about.

"I've been reading up on the First Ladies," she said, "and they always have something they're crusading for. Y'know — keeping America beautiful, reading, women's rights, and stuff."

"Is there some cause you want to crusade for?" I asked.

"Well, I was thinking, do you know how many silkworms die to make a silk blouse?"

"I have no idea, Chelsea."

"Lots!" she exclaimed.

"So you want people to boycott silk clothes?" It seemed like a weird cause to me.

"No!" she exclaimed, horrified. "I *love* silk clothes! I want to lead a crusade in favor of better conditions for those poor silkworms."

At first I thought she was putting me on, but the vacant look in her eyes told me she was absolutely serious. For all I know, silkworms are an endangered species.

"I say go for it, Chelsea," I said. "If you believe in a cause, you have to fight for it."

Mom and Dad could no longer pretend I was just fooling around. When Dad knocked on my bedroom door one night at bedtime and asked if we could have a little talk, I was surprised. The last time we had a man-to-man, I had just run over his vegetable garden with the snowblower.

Dad sat down on my bed and fiddled with the globe on my night table.

"I don't know much about politics, Judd," he said. "All I know is cardboard boxes. But somehow, I figure they're pretty much the same."

This I wanted to hear.

"When I sell a customer a pallet of boxes, I want those boxes to be strong. That's the main thing. If the boxes are weak and fall apart, that customer will never buy a box from me again."

"The president has to be strong too, right, Dad?"

"Right. But it's not good enough to *just* be strong. A box has to have other good qualities. It has to hold lots of stuff. It has to stack easily. It can't weigh too much. You have to be able to put it together quickly. And it has to be labeled clearly so people know exactly what's inside it."

"A president has to be a lot like a box, right, Dad?"

"In a way, yes."

For just about the first time in my life, Dad and I were communicating . . . in an odd sort of way.

"Dad?" I asked. "What would you do if customers really liked a box, but you knew perfectly well that the box was poor quality?"

"Simple," he replied instantly. "I'd sell him the box."

"Even though you know it's not right?"

"The customer is *always* right, Judd," he said. "That's the first rule of selling. You've got to give the customers what they want."

"But what if the customers are stuck with a piece of garbage?"

"That's *their* problem," he explained as he got up from the bed. "They get what they pay for. Maybe next time they'll use a little sense and pick a better box."

"Thanks, Dad," I said. He flipped off my light and I thought about that before falling asleep.

17.
★ Let the Kid Run! ★

It says right there in the Constitution . . .

"No Person except a natural born Citizen, or a Citizen of the United States, at the time of the Adoption of this Constitution, shall be eligible to the Office of President; neither shall any Person be eligible to that Office who shall not have attained the Age of thirty five Years, and been fourteen Years a Resident within the United States."

After the Associated Press article appeared, lots of newspapers ran follow-up stories that included that passage from the Constitution. They said my candidacy was nothing more than a big joke, because by law no twelve-year-old could be president of the United States.

But Lane didn't think it was a joke.

"The Constitution can be changed, y'know," he said as we settled in for our next strategy session at the tree house, which we had renamed *Tranquility Base.*

"Yeah, right," I scoffed. "We'll just go to Washington, sneak in there with some Wite-Out, and get rid of the part that says the president has to be thirty-five years old."

"No, Moon. Haven't you heard of constitutional amendments?"

"Sure I have," I said, not very sure what they were. "The Bill of Rights and stuff."

"The Bill of Rights is the first ten amendments to the Constitution," Lane explained. "There have been twenty-seven altogether."

"They changed the Constitution twenty-seven times!?"

"Yeah. See, the guys who wrote the Constitution knew the world was gonna change. They figured that if the Constitution couldn't be changed with it, the people of the future might weird out and have another revolution. So the Fifteenth Amendment gave people the right to vote regardless of race. The Nineteenth gave women the right to vote, and the Twenty-sixth gave eighteen-year-olds the right to vote."

"How do you know so much, Lane?"

"I read. I study. I learn. You should try it sometime, Moon."

"So how *do* you change the Constitution?"

Lane pulled out our history textbook and leafed through it until he found the passage in the Constitution he was looking for.

"Listen to this, Moon," he read. *"'The Congress, whenever two-thirds of both Houses shall deem it necessary, shall propose Amendments to this Constitution.'"*

He ran his finger down a few lines until he came to the key words. "Oh, here it is . . . *'when ratified by the Legislatures of three-fourths of the several States.'* So two-thirds of the Congress has to propose the amendment, and then the legislatures of three-fourths of the states have to vote in favor of it."

It didn't seem very likely that could ever happen, but the next day a very interesting article appeared on the editorial page of the *New York Times.* . . .

LET THE KID RUN!

By Louis Bixby

The recent presidential candidacy of young Judson Moon of Madison, Wisconsin, has been treated like a national joke in the press. Everyone knows the president of the United States must be

35 years old, so why doesn't this little boy go back to his lemonade stand and leave this important political stuff to us grown-ups?

I have one thing to say about that — let the kid run!

It is time for someone to propose a constitutional amendment to eliminate all age restrictions on running for political office.

This is a free country, last time I looked. All of us have the right to assemble, say or publish anything we want, choose our religion, and enjoy all the other unalienable rights granted in the Constitution and the Bill of Rights. Shouldn't we all have the right to run for political office?

Why is a 35-year-old man — or woman — qualified to be president but a 34-year-old is not? Perhaps the best person to run the country is 30 years old, or even 20 years old.

Who knows? Maybe the best person to lead us is 12 years old. Probably not. But shouldn't that young person have the right to try?

The right to run for office should not be withheld due to sex, race, or age. Judson Moon should have the right to run for president if he wants to. If the kid gets trounced, as he most certainly will, it will be a valuable life lesson for him. And perhaps for us all.

The media had sort of lost interest in the Moon & June campaign after the first wave of publicity, but this was like a match had been dropped into a pool of gasoline. The next day you couldn't turn on the radio without hearing people arguing about the "lemonade stand amendment," as they were calling it.

Some callers would chant "LET THE KID RUN! LET THE KID RUN!" and hang up. Others would say how children don't have the maturity, intelligence, or experience to handle a position of responsibility.

"I've got a twelve-year-old son," one lady commented, "and he can't even drink soup without dribbling it all over his shirt!"

"Thank God that lady's kid ain't runnin' for president!" another caller cracked.

The newspaper columnists jumped into the debate. Celebrities were asked to take a stand on the issue. Picket lines formed outside state capitals with people marching around holding LET THE KID RUN! signs.

USA Today took a poll and found that 64% of all Americans and 99% of all kids felt there should be a constitutional amendment eliminating all age restrictions on running for political office. Congress debated the issue on C-SPAN, and the nation was glued to the tube like we had landed an astronaut on Mars or something.

The children of America decided it was up to *them* to get this amendment passed. At first they protested peacefully at home and at school. Then things started to get ugly.

All across America, kids refused to clean up their rooms unless their parents supported the lemonade stand amendment. They stopped putting their clothes in the hamper. They swallowed their food without chewing it well first.

They refused to bundle up when they went outside. They went swimming immediately after eating. Some of them even ate *while* they were swimming — the ultimate act of defiance.

Newspapers reported that vegetable sales were way down at supermarkets. Kids were simply refusing to eat them.

Lane loved it. He seemed to really enjoy the fact that America was doing something in response to *us*.

Me, I didn't even care anymore. To tell you the truth, I was getting sick of running for president. I was beginning to feel like I was only doing it to please Lane. Running for president wasn't a goof anymore, and it wasn't fun anymore, either.

I couldn't go anywhere without being followed. Reporters were permanently camped out in the lot across the street from my house. Every time our front door would open, they'd rush over, waving their cameras and notebooks and microphones.

My parents, aunts, uncles, and cousins were being hassled for interviews. Mrs. Syers couldn't sit on her porch anymore without holding a press conference. Everybody I ever knew was being asked to describe what I was like.

One day, as a joke, I opened up the front door, poked my head out, and screamed at the reporters across the street, "Give me liberty or give me death!"

The next day headlines appeared in all the papers — **MOON CAN'T TAKE THE PRESSURE!** and **MOON IS LOONEY!** and **JUDSON PUT ON SUICIDE WATCH!** It was crazy.

In the end, public opinion convinced the Senate and House of Representatives that the issue had to be brought up for a vote. Three weeks after the editorial appeared in the *New York Times*, the legislatures of forty-two states ratified Amendment XXVIII to the Constitution . . .

"The right of citizens of the United States to run for elected office in any primary or other election shall not be denied or abridged by the United States or any state on account of age."

Whether I wanted to or not, I was officially in the race for president of the United States.

18.
★ Pols and Polls ★

Naturally, I was not the *only* person running for president of the United States. President George White was hoping to be reelected for a second term, of course. He's a Republican from Ohio, an older guy with big jowly cheeks that wiggle when he talks.

President White was an okay president, I guess. He hadn't gotten America into any wars, or at least any *world* wars, during his four years in office.

A lot of people don't like him, though. Before he was elected, he had promised he was going to lower taxes, balance the budget, and solve all of America's problems. But three years into his presidency, we seemed to have all the same problems and a few new ones, too.

The Democrats seemed to be against everything President White did simply because he was a Republican. Republicans were always criticizing him because they said he wasn't Republican *enough*, whatever that meant.

Sometimes I think people didn't like President White simply because he was the president and they *weren't*.

To make things worse for the president, in January during a ceremony on the White House lawn, his dog went to the bathroom on the ambassador from New Zealand. It was pretty hilarious, and the video of it got something like ten million views on YouTube.

Some commentators said the president can't be expected to manage the country when he can't even manage his own dog.

Anyway, his approval rating went way down after that incident.

The Democratic challenger was Senator Herbert Dunn of West Virginia. You'd recognize him right away because his hair looks like it was made of Styrofoam and surgically fused to his head. Lane and I always say he must comb his hair with a blowtorch.

Senator Dunn was always attacking President White, saying his policies were leading to the decline and fall of civilization and stuff like that. He was angry all the time. A real downer. I couldn't believe anyone would ever vote for him, but he'd been a Senator for about a hundred years, so people must like him. In West Virginia, anyway.

To be perfectly honest, I thought President White and Senator Dunn were a couple of windbags.

In February, *USA Today* took a poll of the American people and this was the result . . .

President White: 53%

Senator Dunn: 43%

Judson Moon: 1%

Other: 3%

"One percent of the vote!" I complained to Mrs. Syers. "That's pathetic! We're doing even worse than Other!"

"Honey," she said, "do you realize a hundred million people are gonna vote on November seventh? You get one percent of that and you got a million votes! A million grown-ups who would vote for you, a snot-nosed, twelve-year-old kid, to be president of the United States! Think about that, child!"

Meanwhile, the money kept pouring in from kids all over America. Poor Gus hurt his back lugging all those sacks to my house every day. In March, he turned in his resignation to the post office. Somebody told me Gus had decided to enter politics himself.

I came home from school one day and there were a dozen or so kids helping out with all the mail, working like little gerbils. Lane called them his "Moonies."

"How'd you get them to do this?" I asked Lane.

"I promised them you would establish a minimum weekly allowance for kids," he replied.

"I can't do that! That's their parents' decision!"

"It's just a *campaign* promise, Moon," he said, as if I was dumb. "You don't have to actually *do* it."

By April, Lane said we had enough money to buy some air time and do TV commercials. This was my favorite part about running for president. I'm a natural ham, and it was really cool to shoot the commercials and watch them on TV.

Mrs. Syers and I made a whole bunch of goofy commercials together, but the one I liked best I did by myself. It was shot at the local high school football field. I started at the one-yard line to show that I had one percent of the vote so far. As I talked, I walked upfield with a football in my arm. Lane and I made up this script . . .

"Hi. My name is Judson Moon and I'm running for president. I know a lot of you out there think that's crazy. You're saying a twelve-year-old kid knows nothing about politics. And you know what? You're absolutely right! I don't know anything!"

The script called for me to pause for a moment at the ten-yard line while some guy tried to tackle me. I threw him a hip fake and he flew by me. Then I continued . . .

"I don't know how to raise your taxes or waste it on things America doesn't need. I don't know how to make secret deals with nutty foreign dictators. I don't know how to ruin our environment. I don't know how to pander to special interest groups. I don't know

how to get us into a war. I wouldn't even know where to begin."

I paused at the twenty-yard line to evade another tackle. Then came the big finish . . .

"Look, I'm just a kid. I don't know anything. That's why you should vote for me on November seventh. Now if you'll excuse me, I've got to run."

At that point a bunch of grown-ups start chasing me down the field — politician types, lawyers holding briefcases, ex-hippies, criminals with knives, housewives, soldiers, terrorists. I break tackles left and right and fake them all out of their shoes. Finally, I high-step over the goal line and spike the ball.

As I was doing my dance in the end zone, a voiceover went, "Vote for Moon. He doesn't know anything."

I just wanted to get a few laughs. But the commercial must have struck a nerve with the American people, because the day after it aired, I shot up to ten percent in the polls.

Some of that gain was at the expense of President White, whose dog happened to bite a little boy during a White House tour. The poor kid had to get stitches in his leg. It was all over the news. I think a lot of people felt so bad about the boy that they switched their votes from White to me.

I felt sorry for the president. It wasn't his fault that his dog was out of control. He was in a tough spot. If he got rid of the dog, people would say he was only doing it to win the election.

But that was *his* problem. We were six months away from Election Day, and the polls showed us at . . .

President White: 43%

Senator Dunn: 43%

Judson Moon: 10%

Other: 4%

At least I was beating "Other."

19.
★ The Virtual Candidate ★

When school let out in June, Lane and I were able to devote ourselves to the campaign full-time. That's when we discovered a secret weapon we didn't even know we had.

The two of us went on the internet one night. I changed my usual handle from JMOON to JSUN so people wouldn't know who I was. We clicked over to some comment sections to see what people were chatting about.

Astonishingly, the screen was filled with people talking about me . . .

```
TinCan: Moon is the one!
Ox: I told my mom I would run
away unless she voted for Moon.
KitKatK: fyi, moon rally in
boston tomorrow at 3:00 . . . tell
everyone u know!
BigDog: Moon is our only hope.
```

```
CarGirl: Down with grown-ups!
HHOK: :-)
Coboe: Moon rules! Yessssssssss!
TNX KitKatK!
Wolf: MOONMOONMOONMOONMOONMOON-
MOONMOON!
```

It went on and on like that. Just for the fun of it, I typed this . . .

```
JSUN: Put an "R" in the middle
of Moon and you'll know what he
is.
```

In seconds, the screen was filled with people flaming me, telling me to get off the site, threatening me, and typing all kinds of vile things. Not a single person online had a negative word to say about Judson Moon.

We jumped around from Facebook to Twitter to Tumblr to see what people had to say about me. Lane's brother was older than thirteen so we could use his accounts. Each of these networks had millions of subscribers, and it was the same thing wherever we looked. Those same kids who were holding yard sales and selling lemonade were burning up the nation's wireless networks trying to whip up support for the Moon & June team by modem.

Some kids established web sites where people could download photos of me and Mrs. Syers, read our life stories, hear us speak, and find out how to start a petition to get us on the ballot in their state.

While President White and Senator Dunn were wasting their time visiting flag factories and giving speeches to try and get themselves noticed, I was campaigning where the people actually were — glued to their computer screens.

And the best part was, I didn't even have to do the work! My supporters were in cyberspace campaigning *for* me. There were millions of Moonies out there.

The work kids were doing online was definitely having an effect. The election was getting closer, and every day my ranking in the polls climbed a few points higher. By September, this was the way we stood . . .

President White: 33%

Senator Dunn: 39%

Judson Moon: 24%

Other: 4%

20.
Moon, You Don't *Have*
★ Any Opinions! ★

I was over at Lane's house when he flipped
on the news and we saw Chelsea Daniels's face
fill the screen. She and a group of her friends
were marching around the state capitol carrying
signs that said "S.O.S." on them.

"Save our silkworms!" they were chanting.
"Save our silkworms!"

The reporter pulled Chelsea aside and asked
her how she and I got along.

"Oh, Judson and I have our little spats like any
other couple," she said. "But he always finds a
way to patch things up. If we can settle our little
differences, I'm sure he can bring our country
together, too. That's the kind of person he is.
I'm sure he'll be a wonderful president. And I'm
really looking forward to being First Lady. Save
our silkworms! Save our silkworms!"

"She hardly knows me!" I said disgustedly. "We've never even spent five minutes together!"

"I'm telling you, Moon," Lane said, "that girl has the potential to go far."

We turned off the set and Lane dropped a bombshell — the League of Women Voters had invited me to debate President White and Senator Dunn live on national television a week before Election Day. Immediately, I started to panic.

"Debate those guys?" I said. "I can't even talk my parents into raising my allowance. Can't we just make a video and send it in?"

"Stop worrying so much," Lane said. "I've got a plan."

Lane always seemed to have a plan. He flipped on his laptop and clicked open a file titled "Debate Strategy."

On the left side of the screen was a long list of all the "hot button" issues Americans are always arguing about. On the right side were numbers indicating how Americans feel about each issue. He had downloaded the data from the latest Gallup Poll.

It looked like this . . .

	FAVOR	OPPOSED
• Affirmative action	50	41
• Stricter gun control	40	50
• Nuclear power	71	24
• Death penalty	67	29

And it went on like that for dozens of issues.

"It's simple," Lane explained. "This is how the average American feels about every important issue. All you have to do is memorize a paragraph about each issue that reflects that opinion. Average Americans will agree with you and they should vote for you."

"But what if my opinion is different from the average American's?" I asked Lane.

"You have opinions, Moon?" he asked with a sneer.

"Sure I have opinions!"

"Then tell me," Lane asked. "Where do you stand on endangered species?"

"Well, if they're endangered I wouldn't stand on them."

"Seriously now. No jokes."

I thought about it for a moment. "We've got to protect animals that are endangered so they don't become extinct," I said.

"Okay," Lane replied. "Would you protect some owls if it meant hundreds of loggers would lose their jobs?"

"Human loggers?" I stammered. "I guess not."

"Okay, what's your position on gun control, Moon?"

"I'm definitely in favor," I replied confidently. "If we get guns off the streets, fewer people will be shot and killed."

"But Moon, the Bill of Rights specifically gives citizens the right to bear arms."

"Oh," I replied. "Well, if that's in the Bill of Rights, then people should have the right to own a gun."

"You can't take both sides on every issue, Moon!"

"Why not?" I complained. "I can *see* both sides of every issue."

"You look wishy-washy," Lane said. "The public wants its leaders to have strong opinions."

"But what if *both* sides of an issue have a good argument?"

"Then you follow the opinions on the computer," he said, gesturing toward the numbers on the screen. "Those are the opinions the public wants you to take. People vote for politicians to represent them. So doesn't it make sense that the politician's opinion should be the same as the public's opinion?"

"That feels backward to me," I said. "I think the president should form an opinion first and inspire the public to agree with that opinion."

"Moon, you don't *have* any opinions!"

He was right, I suppose. Taking sides has always been a problem with me. I can form an opinion, but as soon as somebody comes along and explains the opposite view, I change my mind. The last person I speak with always sounds right. Maybe that's why people like me.

Lane and I spent the next three weeks cramming for the debate. He wrote out my opinions on all the major issues and I memorized them. I didn't learn a whole lot about the issues, but I learned which ones America was in favor of and which ones America opposed.

Lane would grill me by firing questions at me repeatedly — "What should we do about illegal immigration? Unemployment? Medicare? The minimum wage?" I had all the answers on index cards. It was hard to keep everything straight in my head.

Boning up for the debate was much tougher than school, which I was missing more and more of as October went by and the debate got closer.

21.
★ Time to Panic ★

With my army of Moonies all over the country working on our behalf, Moon & June kept rising in the polls. We were just ten points behind President White and five points behind Senator Dunn on the day of the big debate.

Lane and I took a limo out to Chicago that morning and checked into the Palmer House hotel. What I found most amazing was that everywhere I went, people knew me. I had hardly traveled out of Madison in my life, and everybody in Chicago knew me!

People in the airport rushed over to shake my hand. The hotel staff treated me like a visiting dignitary. Kids on the street looked at me like I was a rock star.

The debate was two hours away. I started putting on my gray sport jacket and Lane stopped me.

"Gray is boring," he said, picking out a dark blue jacket and bright red-striped tie. "The camera will love you in this. Wear colors of authority."

I started to protest, but decided against it. Lane had gotten us this far. It wouldn't be fair to start calling the shots myself now.

Lane called a limo to take us to McCormick Place, a convention center where the debate was to be held. Security was tight. There were police and Secret Service agents everywhere, talking into their sleeves, constantly scanning the crowd for potential troublemakers.

The thought crossed my mind that it would be cooler to be a Secret Service agent than to be the president.

When we got inside, we were escorted to a room for our last-minute preparations before air time.

"This is it, Moon," Lane said. "What you say tonight can put us over the top. You can do it. I know you can." He sounded like my Little League coach.

I was nervous as a cat in a vet's waiting room, and it showed. Sweat was coming through my shirt. I couldn't stand still.

"Relax," Lane kept telling me. "Take a deep breath. Remember what I told you. Don't put your hands in your pockets. Don't look at your watch. Make eye contact at all times."

"With who, the moderator?"

"No, with the camera," he said. "You want to connect with the people of America."

I tried to go over my opinions on the issues. There were so many facts buzzing around my head that I started mixing everything up. I felt like my brain was overloading, and the circuit breakers were shutting the system down.

I started to panic. I forgot what affirmative action was. I couldn't remember if I was for or against gun control. I could barely think of my name.

What a time for my mind to go blank!

And what a time for somebody to knock on the door and usher me to the podium.

I was in a fog. I barely noticed President White and Senator Dunn smiling at me from their podiums. The director stood before us and whispered . . .

"We're on the air in five . . . four . . . three . . . two . . . one . . . lights, camera . . ."

22.
★ The Great Debate ★

As I stood behind my podium and looked at the president of the United States fifteen feet away, a thought hit me that should have hit me about ten months ago.

Who am I fooling?

I don't have opinions on any important issues, I thought to myself. I have no business being here. I only wanted to run for president as a goof. I never thought it would go this far. I can't run a country.

I'm like one of those idiots who runs on the field in the middle of a baseball game!

But it was too late to back out. I couldn't just walk off the stage.

It was at that moment that I figured out my only option was to sabotage my own candidacy.

I decided to do what I always do when I'm in a jam — play it for laughs and act like a jerk. Maybe America will forgive me for wasting its valuable time. Maybe people will say boys will be boys and let me go back to my normal life.

The League of Women Voters, who sponsored the debate, had decided on a format designed to prevent candidates from rambling on and on — each candidate would be asked a question by members of a panel and have twenty seconds to complete his answer. The three of us would take turns fielding questions.

The moderator introduced President White, Senator Dunn, and me. The panel of journalists fired the first question at Senator Dunn and the next one at the president. Each of them gave a very thoughtful, rehearsed, and (to me, anyway) boring response. Then everyone looked at me.

"Mr. Moon," I was asked, "a third-party candidate has never won the presidency. What makes you think your Lemonade Party can?"

Lane knew I would be asked that question,

and he had written a good answer for it. But I couldn't remember what it was. So I improvised.

"I look at it this way," I said. "The two-party system is an improvement on a one-party system. Therefore, three parties should be an improvement on two parties. Americans love parties, and I believe the more parties we have the better. I would start a fourth party if I could, but I can only start one party at a time. So, in conclusion, I say . . . let's party, America!"

The place erupted. The studio audience was screaming. Half of them were laughing their heads off. The other half were demanding that I be removed from the auditorium. The panel of journalists stared at me, openmouthed. It took a while for order to be restored.

As soon as I finished giving that answer, a sense of calm came over my body. I stopped sweating. I wasn't nervous anymore. It was as if a weight had been lifted off my shoulders. I felt like I was back in the school cafeteria, goofing on Arthur Krantz and his jerky friends.

The three candidates took turns. Every time the panel of journalists threw a question at me, I threw the answer right back. . . .

Q: You're on record as saying your first official act as president will be to abolish homework. What will your second official act be?

A: To abolish making beds. Why make a bed in the morning? You're only going to sleep in it again that night.

Q: What do you plan to do about jobs?

A: I plan to get one as soon as my term as president is over.

Q: Which president do you most admire, and why?

A: Grover Cleveland. Because he became president despite the fact that he was named after a character on Sesame Street.

Q: How do you feel about school prayer?

A: Every morning I pray that school will be closed.

Q: What do you intend to do about teenage pregnancy?

A: My dad says we're going to sit down and have a talk about that, but he keeps putting it off.

Q: It takes a tremendous amount of desire to become president. Do you have the fire in the belly?

A: Yeah, it must have been those tacos I ate for dinner.

Q: What's the toughest part about running for president?

A: Learning not to pick my nose in public.

Q: What do you think we should do about hazardous waste?

A: I'd suggest you try a strong laxative.

That ought to do it, I thought to myself. I couldn't say anything more disgusting, juvenile, or unpresidential than that. Nobody could *possibly* take me seriously as a candidate for president.

President White and Senator Dunn stood there during my answers. Both of them were flustered. When the journalists asked them a question, they fumbled all over the place trying to look dignified. I guess they weren't used to obnoxious kids.

For our final statements, all three of us were asked to address one issue we would be likely to face as president — how to achieve lasting peace in the Middle East.

The president gave a little speech about how he had formed deep relationships with all the Mideast leaders over the last four years. Senator Dunn said that the United States had to back up its friends in the event of a conflict.

I didn't have any strong opinion on the subject, and I couldn't think of a good wisecrack. So I told a little story.

"One time I was at a baseball card show and some kids got into a big argument over whose cards belonged to whom. I stepped in the middle of it and looked over their collections. I told one kid that if he gave the second kid his Ryan Howard rookie card and the other kid gave him two Matt Holliday cards, they would be even. I told the third kid that if he gave each of the other kids his Cliff Lee and Tim Lincecum cards, they would probably give him the Robinson Cano and Joey Votto cards that he wanted. To make a long story short, they made all the swaps and everybody was happy afterward. So I think I could keep everybody in the Middle East happy the same way."

"I don't believe the Israelis or Palestinians collect baseball cards," the moderator chuckled.

"Well, maybe they should," I said. "It's better to fight over cards than it is to fight over countries."

And that was the end of the debate. The moderator came over and thanked all three of us for participating. I shook hands with the president and even got his autograph.

When I came off the stage, Lane was sitting on

the floor with his knees up and his head buried in his hands. He looked like a kid whose pet had died or something.

"I'm sorry, Lane," I said. "I guess I just don't have the fire in the belly to be president."

He didn't say a word to me on the ride back to Madison. He just stared out the window.

23.
★ The Runaway Train ★

I had trouble sleeping after the debate and got up very early. I went downstairs to get the morning paper. The reporters camped out across the street weren't even awake yet.

The headline on the front page nearly knocked me over:

MOON WINS DEBATE, SURGES AHEAD!
By Ralph Hammelbacher

12-year-old Judson Moon cleverly turned the tables on President White and Senator Dunn last night, shocking the nation in the most freewheeling evening of political debate in memory.

Instead of engaging in a conventional debate, the youngster used the opportunity to thumb his nose at the political system in front of the entire nation.

President White and Senator Dunn were reduced to dumbfounded onlookers as Moon deftly and hilariously controlled the proceedings with snappy retorts and off-the-wall opinions that threw his opponents off their stride.

"Moon knew exactly what he was doing," said political analyst Morton Fishwick. "He knew he couldn't beat his opponents by debating the issues, so he made the issues go away. I've got to hand it to him. It was brilliant strategy on the kid's part."

In telephone polls taken immediately after the debate, an overwhelming majority of people — young and old — named Moon as the victor.

With just five days until the election, the Moon & June steamroller has a three point lead over President White, according to an Associated Press poll. Senator Dunn trails by seven points.

Mom was so happy, she invited just about everyone we'd ever known over to the house to celebrate. Lane was happy again and even congratulated me for relying on my "political instincts" instead of taking his advice. My folks beamed. Arthur Krantz steamed.

June Syers just looked at me with that look that said she'd known it all along. Abby called and said she was too busy to make the party, but I think she didn't come because she knew Chelsea would be there.

Chelsea had her arm snaked around my elbow like we were stuck together. She had to leave early, though, explaining that she had to begin the long and arduous task of shopping for clothes she would wear as First Lady.

I pretty much sat there, dazed, during the whole party. I couldn't figure out how I'd messed up messing up the debate.

The candidacy was like a runaway train now. Nothing could stop my momentum. I had done everything short of dropping my pants to wreck my chances of winning the election. It didn't work. Unless something disastrous happened quickly, I was going to be the next president of the United States.

And then something disastrous happened.

24.
★ Moongate ★

In the middle of the celebration at my house, I received a phone call from Pete Guerra, my reporter friend who wrote the first article about the lemonade stand that started the whole ball rolling.

"Congratulations," Pete said. "That was quite a show you put on last night."

"Thanks, Pete. Listen, I can't talk now. There are a lot of people over here."

"Lemme ask you one quick question, Judson."

"Go ahead, Pete."

"Did you break into some kid's locker and steal his term paper when you were in fourth grade?"

I remembered the incident. It was that jerk Arthur Krantz. He had put a sign that said KICK ME on my backpack, so I stole his term paper and threw it down the sewer. It wasn't any big deal.

"Yeah, Pete, I did that. Why?"

"Just checking," Guerra said. "Enjoy your party."

I forgot all about it until the next morning, when Lane called early and shouted, "Did you see today's paper?!"

I ran outside. The reporters swarmed all over me, sticking microphones in my face. "Is it true? Will you drop out of the race?"

I dashed inside with the paper and read the story that was splashed across the front page.

MOONGATE! YOUNG CANDIDATE ROCKED BY SCANDAL

By Pete Guerra

Judson Moon burglarized another student's locker and deliberately destroyed important papers, according to an informed source. With just three days remaining until Election Day, the young candidate is faced with a personal scandal that may derail his presidential hopes.

The incident took place two years ago. After an argument with the other student, Moon used a metal ruler to pry open the locker. Several papers were removed and never recovered. It is unclear at this time what information was on those papers.

Principal Harold Berlin is cooperating with the FBI on the investigation.

"If Judson Moon did this," he says, "I would have to reconsider whether I would want him to be the leader of our country."

Other problems are beginning to surface for the young candidate, who up until now has seemed like the perfect all-American boy. It has been learned that aspiring "First Lady" Chelsea Daniels did not even know Moon's name until he decided to run for president.

"He thought he'd have a better chance of winning if he was with a cute babe," one student revealed.

Also, it has been revealed that Moon changed the name of his parakeet to make it more acceptable to the American public. "Cuddles's" real name is apparently "Snot."

So Booger Boy Krantz went and gabbed to the press. That jerk! He would do anything to bring me down.

"Is it true?" demanded Lane when I got back on the phone.

"Sure it's true," I replied. "So what?"

"It's going to cost us the election, that's what! I worked so hard to make the public think you're an innocent kid who doesn't have a bad bone in his body. And now *this*. What was on those papers you stole?"

"It was Arthur Krantz's stupid term paper. I threw it down the sewer."

"What was the term paper about?"

"The Constitution and the Bill of Rights."

"You threw the Constitution down a sewer?!"

"It was just a goof!"

"That's the problem, Moon. Everything is a goof with you!" Lane slammed down the phone.

The press jumped all over the "Moongate" scandal. I tuned into a couple of talk radio shows and it seemed like all the people who had been saying how wonderful I was now wanted to ride me out of town on a rail.

I pretended to be upset about what happened, but on the inside I was secretly happy. Thanks to Booger Boy Krantz, I found a way to lose the election.

Still, it bothered me that Pete Guerra wrote the story. I didn't care about being president, but I wasn't happy that everybody knew about Snot and Chelsea. It made me look like a phony.

I picked up the phone and dialed Guerra's number.

"Pete," I said. "I thought you were my friend."

"Remember what I told you at the beginning, Moon? *Nobody* is your friend. Everybody wants a piece of you, and that includes me. I'm a reporter. My job is not to help you become president. My job is to find great stories people want to read so they'll buy my paper."

"Breaking into a kid's locker is a great story?" I asked. "Changing my parakeet's name is a great story?"

"If you're the presidential front-runner those are *terrific* stories!" Pete exclaimed. "Like I said, Moon. America chews up celebrities and spits 'em out. And America is about to clear its throat with you."

Lane was furious at me, but he wasn't ready to give up the fight. There were still two days until the election. He decided our only chance to save the campaign was for me to go on national TV and talk directly to the American people.

I didn't want to do it. "Look," I pleaded with Lane, "let's just forget about it. I never really wanted to be president anyway. It was just a —"

"A goof. I know, Moon. Everything is a goof with you. But when we got started on this thing, we agreed on one thing — I'm in charge of the campaign. After Election Day, you're in charge. But up until then, I call the shots. I tell you what to do, what to wear, what to say and when to say it. Remember? I didn't work my tail off for the last year to see you quit two days before the election. You owe me, Moon."

I may have lied and faked my way through the campaign, but I am a boy of my word. I agreed to go on national TV and read a statement.

"You've got to read it word for word," Lane warned me. "No improvising. No jokes. No goofing around."

"Word for word," I agreed.

25.
★ Word for Word ★

The Moongate scandal definitely had an impact across America. People had thought I was squeaky clean. They didn't want to hear that I used dirty tricks. Moon & June dropped ten points in the polls instantly. President White was back in the lead, with Senator Dunn and me five points behind.

Lane drained the last dollars from the money we raised to buy ten minutes of air time during halftime of *Monday Night Football.* He wanted to make sure all of America was watching. It was the night before Election Day.

We did the filming in front of my house, with my parents standing behind me. Lane dressed me in a plain gray suit. "I want you to look boring," he said. Just before the camera started rolling, Lane told my dad to put a hand on my shoulder.

"My fellow Americans," I read somberly off the cue cards Lane held up, "in the last few days a story came out that I broke into someone's locker and stole some papers. I can understand if you have second thoughts about voting for me. I wouldn't want to have a president who did that sort of thing, and I'm sure you wouldn't either.

"I'm here tonight to come clean with America. Yes, I admit it. I broke into Arthur Krantz's locker and threw his term paper down the sewer. It was a childish prank.

"I know that what I did was wrong. I was younger then. I'm much more mature now. I learned a valuable lesson from this experience and I will never, *ever* do anything like that again. You have my word on that.

"And yes, my parakeet's name is Snot. I thought the American people would not accept that, so I changed it to Cuddles.

"One other thing I probably should tell you, because if I don't they'll probably be saying this about me, too. I did get something, a gift. A man down in Texas heard that I would like to have a dog. And, believe it or not, one day I got a message that the post office had a package for me. I went down to get it. You know what it was? It was a little cocker spaniel dog, in a crate that had been sent all the way from Texas — black and white, spotted. I named it Chester. And you know, I love that dog. And I just want to say this, right now, that regardless of what they say about it, I'm gonna keep it. Thank you, and enjoy the rest of the game."

That was it. I took off the microphone and breathed a big sigh of relief. The campaign was finally over. Lane shook my hand and told me I did a great job.

"Where did you come up with that bit about Chester?" I asked him. "It was really corny."

"I didn't write it."

"Who did?"

"Richard Nixon."

"The president?" I asked. "Isn't he dead?"

"He wrote it in 1952, when he was running for vice president," Lane explained. "Nixon had received some shady campaign contributions and Eisenhower was going to drop him and pick another person to be his running mate. Then Nixon went on national TV right after Milton Berle's show and made this speech. His dog was named Checkers and the speech came to be called the Checkers speech. It saved his career."

"You mean I just gave Nixon's Checkers speech?"

"Well, I changed a word or two," Lane said, with a wicked smile on his face.

26.
★ Election Day ★

Election Day is always the first Tuesday after the first Monday in November. When I woke up that morning, I had a bad feeling in the pit of my stomach. If the Checkers speech worked for me like it worked for Richard Nixon, I might actually *win* the election.

The overnight polls showed that the speech hit home with at least *some* Americans. Moon & June jumped up a few points and President White dropped down a few. CNN said the race was too close to call.

Senator Dunn had dropped down to a distant third. It looked like it was all over for him.

School was open on Election Day and I decided to go. Staying home all day would only make me more nervous than I already was.

My school is the place where grown-ups in the neighborhood go to vote. Every Election Day, the gym is emptied out and filled with those big voting machines. I always thought of Election Day as a drag, because we wouldn't get to have gym that day.

It was pretty weird seeing all those grown-ups lining up to vote, and thinking that some of them would be voting for *me*. It was the first time I really understood or appreciated that this is how we make important decisions in this country.

It was impossible to pay much attention to school. Everybody was looking at me, asking me how I felt, requesting autographs. The teachers didn't seem to be able to concentrate on their lessons, either.

Chelsea caught up with me after homeroom. "I'm so excited!" she said. "I'm going to wear my red silk dress with the shoulder ruffles to the party tonight!"

"I'm sure you'll look terrific," I said with as much fake enthusiasm as I could muster. Chelsea was really starting to get on my nerves.

Lane had booked the Presidential Suite and

the big ballroom at the fancy Edgewater Hotel for the evening. Just about everybody in town was going to be there to watch the election returns on TV.

Lane and I didn't get the chance to talk until lunchtime. I told him what I'd heard about the latest polls. For the first time, he didn't seem that interested.

"Polls mean nothing at this point," Lane said. "It's the electoral votes that matter now."

I never really understood that whole electoral college thing, so Lane explained it to me. It turns out that each of the fifty states is given one electoral vote for every member it has in Congress. That includes the state's two Senators plus however many members it has in the House of Representatives.

The states with higher populations have more representatives, and more electoral votes. So states like New York, California, Texas, and Pennsylvania have more electoral votes than less populated states like Nevada, Alaska, and Rhode Island.

Lane explained that whichever candidate gets the most votes in a state wins all the electoral votes in that state. And whichever candidate gets 270 or more electoral votes wins the election.

It didn't seem exactly fair to me. A candidate could become president if he just won a few of the big states, even though he lost all the smaller states.

Lane said it was even possible to win the election on electoral votes even if more people voted for the other candidate. In fact, that actually happened in 1824, 1876, 1888, and 2000.

"What if *nobody* gets 270 electoral votes?" I asked.

"Then the House of Representatives votes to decide who will be president."

After school I went home and Mom fussed over me, making food and helping me pick out clothes for the evening. I think it was the longest time I'd ever spent with her when she didn't mention carpet tiles once.

After dinner, Mom, Dad, and I checked into the Presidential Suite at the Edgewater Hotel. Lane was already there, running around, completing last-minute details for the party afterward. June Syers was wheeled in by her kids, who were older than my mom and dad. Mrs. Syers looked great, in a new print dress and lace hat.

All my aunts, uncles, and cousins milled around, scarfing down chips and those little hot dogs wrapped in rolls.

Chelsea looked fabulous in her silk dress, of course. I invited her to stay with us in the Presidential Suite, but she said she was too nervous and would watch the results in the ballroom downstairs. I think she just wanted to be where the most people would see her dress.

Lane's plan was for me to come down to the ballroom as soon as the TV networks declared a winner. He had written two speeches for me — an acceptance speech in case I won, and a concession speech in case I lost.

He also arranged for the hotel to put four TV sets in our room so we could watch ABC, CBS, NBC, and CNN all at the same time. When the polls started to close on the East Coast at 8:00 P.M., we pulled chairs around the glowing screens.

For about an hour, none of the results were in and the announcers filled the time by talking — mostly about *me*. They went on and on about how historic it was for a kid to run for president.

"I have seen a lot of big stories in my career reporting the news," one of the anchormen babbled. "The Kennedy assassination. The Vietnam War. Watergate. Man landing on the moon. The tragedy of September eleventh, 2001. But never in all those years did it ever cross my mind that a child would not only run for president, but ever have a chance of winning the presidency. This is a turning point in the history of the Earth."

Lane and I made gagging noises and pretended to stick our fingers down our throats.

"If the Earth knew it was gonna be around this long," Mrs. Syers said, "it woulda taken better care of itself."

A little after 9:00 o'clock Eastern time the results started coming in. We stopped talking among ourselves and pulled our chairs closer to the screens.

"With thirteen percent of the votes in," the CNN announcer suddenly said, "we are projecting the state of Delaware and its three electoral votes will go to President White."

"Booooo!" everybody hooted, but nobody was too upset. "Three lousy votes," my dad said. "It means nothing."

A few minutes later, the ABC commentator stopped in the middle of a sentence and announced, "We are projecting the state of Maine and its four electoral votes will go to young Judson Moon!"

Everybody yelled and screamed. "We're winning!" my mom shouted. "We're actually *winning*!"

"Calm down," Dad grumbled. "That's just four lousy votes. They mean nothing."

Then the results started *pouring* in. CBS projected President White was the winner in Connecticut. NBC picked me to take New Jersey. President White picked up Vermont, Rhode Island, Florida, and New Hampshire. I won in New York, with its thirty-one big electoral votes.

Senator Dunn won West Virginia's five electoral votes, but he's *from* West Virginia. I figure if you can't win your own state, you must be really pathetic. Outside of West Virginia, he wasn't doing very well. It was going to be White against Moon for all the marbles.

Moon & June pulled ahead of President White in the electoral vote tally, but only slightly. The polls were now closed on the West Coast and it was looking like the election was going to come down to California and its fifty-five electoral votes.

President White would win a state, and then I would win one. Every time a winner was projected, Mrs. Syers would shriek with glee or disappointment depending on whether or not we won the state. Dad was trying not to appear nervous. But he was pacing the floor and mumbling to himself, which he always does when he's uptight.

Lane was very calm and serious. He had his laptop computer with him and he kept recalculating the electoral vote totals every time one of the TV networks projected a winner for a state.

By 11:30 P.M., the results were tabulated from every state except California. All four TV networks said the vote was still too close to call there. I was stuck at 217 electoral votes and the president had 164.

"If we win in California, Moon & June is the winner by two electoral votes," announced Lane.

"If White wins in California, the election is thrown to the House of Representatives to decide."

The voting was over. It was out of our hands. There was no speech anybody could make, no hand anybody could shake that would make a difference. There was nothing to do but sit there and watch.

Sitting there, I felt like I must be in the middle of a dream. This Judson Moon everybody was talking about was some *other* kid. It wasn't me. It was too unbelievable to think that I was actually running for president of the United States. Or that I might actually *win*.

It *had* to be a dream. Or maybe a nightmare. Sometimes it's hard to tell one from the other.

I was shaken from these thoughts when the CNN anchorman suddenly announced, "This just in!" with some urgency in his voice.

Everybody stopped talking.

"At 11:52 P.M., Eastern Standard Time, on November seventh, CNN projects the state of California will go to . . ."

He paused for just a moment to take a breath. "Moon & June! Judson Moon will become the next president of the United States! For the first time in American history —"

I didn't hear the rest. A roar went up in the hotel room. Mom and Dad and Mrs. Syers were all over me, hugging me, kissing me. Car horns blared from the street outside.

"Kings of the hill!" Lane shouted, jumping all over the couch like a maniac. "We did it, Judd! We're kings of the hill!"

I think Lane was happier than anybody. He grabbed me and thanked me for letting him run the campaign. "This is all I ever wanted," he whispered in my ear. "Remember our deal? I'll never tell you what to wear or say or do again. Now *you're* in charge."

I shivered when he said that. *I'm in charge.*

After the commotion had subsided a bit, we all tumbled downstairs to the ballroom where a few thousand people were waiting. When the elevator door opened, a spotlight found me and Mrs. Syers and a deafening roar exploded. Hundreds of red, white, and blue balloons fell from the ceiling. The band struck up "Shine On, Harvest Moon."

Men pummeled me on the back and women kissed me. Some people just reached out and touched me, like I was a religious object.

Lane guided me to the podium and handed me a sheet of paper.

"What does it say?" I asked.

"It's a pretty standard acceptance speech," he said. "The usual patriotic stuff."

I looked out into the crowd. They wouldn't stop cheering. I held up my hands. I shrugged my shoulders. I put my finger to my lips as if to say "Shh!" They kept right on screaming.

I spotted Chelsea in the crowd, clapping as hard as she could without ruining her nails. On the other side of the room I saw Abby, smiling at me like a mom watching her kid at his first piano recital.

It must have been fifteen minutes until the noise level died down enough for me to speak.

"I shouldn't be here," I finally said into the microphone. "It's way past my bedtime."

The ballroom exploded in another roar and I had to wait five more minutes for everybody to quiet down.

"I have a prepared victory speech," I said, "but I'm not going to use it." I glanced at Lane and saw his eyebrows shoot up into his forehead.

"First of all, I want to thank the people who got me here. Mom and Dad, of course. June Syers. Lane Brainard. All the volunteers and kids across America who worked so hard to make this impossible dream happen. And of course, all the people who voted for me."

I paused for a moment to let that sink in. Because I knew that what I was about to say was going to blow their minds.

"I have a question for the grown-ups of America," I said seriously. "Are you out of your *minds*? Are you expecting *me* to enforce the Constitution? I never even *read* it. I was absent from school that day.

"You want *me* as commander in chief of the armed forces? What if somebody attacked the United States? Would you really want *me* in charge? I don't know the difference between North Korea and North Carolina.

"You expect *me* to sign bills into law? You

expect *me* to appoint Supreme Court justices? I'm just a snot-nosed *kid*!"

For once in my life, I wasn't goofing. And it felt good.

"To win this election," I said, "I became everything I always hated. I turned into a liar, a fake, a fraud. The saddest part is, it worked.

"America must be in really bad shape if you elected *me* president. You better get it together and find some qualified people to run this country or we'll all be in big trouble.

"In conclusion," I said, "I hereby *resign* as president-elect of the United States of America."

Have you ever heard three thousand people gasp at the same time? It's really cool. For a second, I thought all the air was going to be sucked out of the ballroom.

It was so quiet you could have heard a pin drop in there, at least until my mom fainted and hit the floor with a thud.

The press were all over me like ants at a picnic. "Does this make Mrs. Syers president?" somebody asked. "Will you reconsider? What about all the kids who worked so hard to get you elected? Are you finished with politics? What are you going to do with the rest of your life?"

"Ladies and gentlemen of the press," I announced, "I don't even know what I'm going to do tomorrow, much less the rest of my life. To use the words of my running mate, June Syers, the future will tell us what will happen when it's good and ready."

As I trotted off the stage, everybody was looking at me like they were dead fish in a fish store.

The first person to come over to me was Lane, of course.

"Once again, your political instincts are brilliant, Moon," he said, clapping a hand on my back. "You make a much better candidate than you would make a president. Perfect career move."

June Syers rolled her wheelchair over to me. "Now I know for *sure* you're crazy, Judson Moon," she said.

"You're probably right, Mrs. Syers."

"Too bad you're out of the race, though," she continued.

"Why?"

" 'Cause you're just the kind of man I would vote for," she said. Considering that she hadn't voted since 1944, I was very flattered.

"Hey," Mrs. Syers said before rolling away. "You promised you'd kiss me on Election Night. So pucker up, big boy!" She wrapped her arms around me and for the life of me I can't figure out how such a tiny little woman could squeeze so hard.

Chelsea Daniels was sobbing uncontrollably, so Lane and I went over to comfort her.

"Hundreds of thousands of silkworms are going to die a horrible death," she bawled, "and I won't be able to do a single thing about it!"

Tears were running down her face, making little dark streams when they dissolved her makeup. Lane pointed to himself to let me know he would take care of Chelsea.

"You know, Chelsea," Lane said, "I've been thinking about you. Have you ever considered entering the Miss America pageant? You have the looks, the personality, and a cause you believe in. I think you can win, and I can help you do it."

"Really?" Chelsea said, dabbing her eyes with a handkerchief and pulling herself together. "But I'm only twelve years old. Don't you have to be eighteen or something?"

"There are ways around that," Lane said, flipping me a wink and leading her away. "Here's what we have to do . . ."

"So long, king of the hill!" I called after him.

Abby came over to me with a big smile on her face. "I don't know much about politics," she said as she straightened my tie, "but that was a *great* speech!"

"You really think so?"

"Oh yeah. I *told* you you'd make a great president, Moon. I just think you make a better kid."

"You're probably right," I said. "Hey, Ab, I was wondering. Maybe you wanna come over tomorrow after school?"

"And do what, Judd?"

"Oh, I don't know. Play a game of *Life* maybe."

"Sounds fabulous!"

★ You Peeked! ★

Nice try. That was pretty clever, going straight to the back of the book to see how the story turned out. But you don't want to spoil the ending for yourself, do you? Now go back to the beginning and read the whole thing.

There are no shortcuts in life.

Learn what America's youngest president does next in

THE KID WHO
★ BECAME ★
PRESIDENT

3.
★ Let's Make a Deal ★

The weatherman had predicted rain in the Washington, D.C., area for Inauguration Day, but as I mounted the podium on the west side of the Capitol Building, the clouds parted to reveal a beautiful, sunny but chilly January day.

As I looked out across the National Mall, I was struck most of all by the people. Thousands and thousands had jammed the grassy area outside the Smithsonian museums that line both sides of the Mall. They spilled out onto Independence Avenue and Pennsylvania Avenue. The sea of faces stretched all the way to the Washington Monument off in the distance.

Flags were everywhere. Enormous ones flying from every building and tiny ones in the hands of little children. Marching bands played enthusiastically. "Yankee Doodle." "The Battle Hymn of the Republic."

As I turned to look at the stands behind the podium, I spotted my mom and dad beaming at me and waving. I wasn't sure how they were going to deal with me being president. All my life they had been in charge of me. Now I would be in charge of . . . *everyone.*

My parents were standing next to Chelsea Daniels — dressed to kill, of course — and her parents.

Mrs. Syers was sitting in her wheelchair behind me, her hands folded in her lap, looking very regal and proud. She had already been sworn in as vice president.

Lane was up in the stands in a corner seat, with a smirk on his face. I wouldn't have been able to get elected president of the student council at school without him, and he knew it.

The rest of the bleachers were filled with dignitaries — senators, members of Congress, Supreme Court justices, the outgoing president, and all the living ex-presidents.

At precisely noon, the chief justice of the

Supreme Court leaned into his microphone and asked, "Mr. Moon, are you prepared to take the oath of office as president of the United States?"

"I am, sir."

The chief justice held up a Bible, the same one George Washington had used when he was sworn in as our country's first president back in 1789. Shivers went up and down my spine as I raised my right hand and repeated those thirty-seven words that change history:

> "I, Judson Moon, do solemnly swear that I will faithfully execute the Office of President of the United States, and will, to the best of my ability, preserve, protect, and defend the Constitution of the United States."

I wasn't old enough to vote. I couldn't legally drive a car. I couldn't take a sip of my dad's beer. But I was president of the United States. I felt like I had to be in the middle of a dream. It couldn't really be happening.

Only in America!

A twenty-one-gun salute echoed off the buildings and a cheer went up from the crowd. Balloons rose into the air. Doves were released. The Marine Band played "Hail to the Chief."

The former president, who was now just an ordinary citizen, shook my hand. "Good luck, President Moon," he said solemnly as he handed me a large brown briefcase. "This is for you. Take good care of it, young man."

Nobody had told me the president was going to give me a *gift*. Considering that I had beaten him in the election, it was very gracious of him. I didn't really like the color of the briefcase, but my mother always told me that when someone gave me a gift I should pretend I loved it, whether I really liked it or not.

"Thank you, Mr. President," I said. "I can hardly wait to use it."

The president looked horrified. The chief justice leaned over and whispered into my ear.

"That briefcase," he said, "contains the instructions for launching nuclear missiles in case there is an attack on the United States. Keep it by your side always."

Oops! One minute into my presidency and I had already goofed! I leaned back to the former president and told him that I hoped I would never have to use his "gift."

When the crowd settled down and everyone in the stands took their seats, I stepped up to the microphone. Lane had worked hard on my Inaugural Address.

"My fellow Americans," I said, hearing the words echo a second after I spoke them. "When I was running for president, I said you should vote for me because I didn't know anything about politics. I didn't know how to raise taxes. I didn't know how to ruin the economy. I didn't know how to get us into a war. I said you should vote for me because I didn't know *anything*."

The crowd chuckled in appreciation.

"Well, that was two months ago, and I'm very proud to say that . . . (Lane told me to pause here) I *still* don't know anything!"

The crowd roared in approval.

"Let's face it," I continued, "I'm a kid. I'm going to need a lot of help from all of you. Kids and grown-ups. Men and women. Rich and poor. People of all races. Will you help me?"

"YESSSSSSSSSSSSSSSSSSSS!" the crowd thundered.

"My fellow Americans. President Theodore Roosevelt gave the country what he called a Square Deal. President Franklin D. Roosevelt gave the country a New Deal. President Truman gave us a Fair Deal. Today I say this to America — Let's make a deal."

Everybody went nuts.

"Here's the deal I offer America — I'll help you all if you all help me. I'm not a Republican, so you Democrats have no reason to oppose me. I'm not a Democrat, so you Republicans have no reason to oppose me. But if we all work together, we can guide our nation together."

There was too much applause to continue, so I let it die down until everybody could hear me.

"Together, we can clean up the environment," I announced. "Together, we can educate children and take care of our senior citizens. Together, we can put an *end* to crime, an *end* to poverty, an *end* to unemployment, an *end* to substance abuse, an *end* to peace in the world."

There was a gasp. I looked at my speech and saw that I had skipped a line.

"I mean, we're going to *have* peace in the world."

A thunderous ovation rolled across the Mall.

"The twentieth century is over, the twenty-first is well under way. We've got a lot of work to do. So, America, I ask you, ARE YOU READY TO RUMMMMMBLE?"

"*YEAHHHHHHHHHHHH!*"

"Let's get it on," I concluded.

They didn't stop applauding for twenty minutes.

MISFITS UNITE!

More madcap antics from
GORDON KORMAN

📖 SCHOLASTIC

www.scholastic.com

GORKORRE